Last Rites

A Last Healer Mystery
By Charles Huss

For my wife, Rose, who is my Katie, my partner in crime.

Chapter 1

In her twelve years working for Channel 23 News, Ashley Taylor had been to many of Milwaukee's seediest locations, but she never felt more nervous than when visiting her mom at work. Her mom had called her that morning and said she had some information that Ashley's station might be interested in.

As Ashley drove past the front of her mom's office, she noticed several men hanging around near the entrance. She didn't feel comfortable walking through the gauntlet, so she drove around to the back of the building and parked in the parking lot.

She entered the Social Services building through the back door and made her way to her mom's office near the front entrance. The door was closed. It had a large, frosted-glass window with her mom's name and title: "Virginia Hall – Senior Case Manager." Ashley was very proud of her mother's work. It was certainly something she couldn't do.

She knocked on the door and opened it a crack. When she saw no clients inside, she opened it all the way. "Hi, Mom."

Ashley's mom looked a lot like Ashley. She was tall with long, blond hair. Like Ashley, she wasn't skinny like a model, but she was attractive. She stood up, walked around her desk, and hugged her daughter. "Hi, Honey. Thanks for coming."

"Anything for you, Mom. What's going on? What's so important?"

"Well, it could be nothing, but it feels like something."

"What feels like something? What do you have?"

She opened her top desk drawer and pulled out a folder. She handed it to Ashley, who opened it and carefully read the first page. She then looked through the rest of it. It contained several photos and reports that Ashley skimmed through. She looked at her mom and asked, "Did you show these to the police?"

"No. There's no proof in there that a crime has been committed. It's all just speculation on my part. The police don't have the resources to chase after speculations."

"Have you spoken to anyone else about this?"

"Just a couple of people in the office here."

"What did they say?"

"Well, one is unsure what I should do, and the other thinks it's all a coincidence."

"I'll be honest, Mom. I'm not sure if this is enough to start an investigation. Even if it was, the station is still short an investigative reporter."

"Why don't we talk about it over lunch? I'll buy. Later, if you feel there is something you can do, I'll make copies for you."

"Okay, Mom. That sounds good."

They went out the back door and walked to Ashley's car. As they were about to get in, someone wearing a ski mask approached, pointed a gun at Virginia Hall, and fired twice. Ashley screamed as she watched the gun turn toward her and fire.

***

Joe opened the front door and picked up Katie. She giggled as he carried her over the threshold. When he put her down, she said, "You already carried me over the threshold two months ago when we bought this house."

"Yes, but this is the first time we have been here as a married couple."

Katie kissed Joe and said, "I love that you are so traditional."

"I was raised in a different time."

"You sure were. Now go get the luggage out of the car."

"Your command is my wish, my dear."

Katie shook her head and said, "Always with the jokes."

That's why you love me," Joe said as he walked out the door.

Katie entered the kitchen and saw a gift basket with wine, assorted cheeses, and crackers. The card attached to it read, "A little something to keep the honeymoon going. Love, Susan, Michael, and Eric."

When Joe returned with the luggage, she showed him the basket and said, "It's from your family. It seems someone raised them right."

"Joe put the suitcases down, took Katie in his arms, and kissed her passionately. After several seconds, she pulled away and said, "Oh, did you think I was talking about you?"

Joe reached down and tickled her side. Katie laughed, and Joe said, "Never forget I know where your ticklish spots are."

"I hate that you are not ticklish," Katie said.

"I have to be better than you at something."

"What are you talking about? You are better than me at everything."

"More experienced, maybe, but not better. I'm certainly not better than you at looking good."

Katie put her arms around Joe and kissed him. "Well, you are better than anyone at making a girl feel good."

"Speaking of feeling good," Joe said. "I think it's time for a healing session."

"Oh, I love those," Katie said as Joe led her to the living room. They sat next to each other on the sofa and held hands. They both closed their eyes as Joe thought of Katie as an extension of his body. Soon, they were connected and could feel each other from the inside. Joe felt for abnormalities inside Katie and soon found one. It was unexpected, and the distraction caused him to lose contact with her.

Katie opened her eyes and asked, "What's wrong?"

"I felt something," Joe said.

"You did? What did you feel?"

"I shouldn't tell you. It would be better if you felt it yourself."

"Is it something bad? Do I need to worry?"

"No. You definitely don't need to worry."

They both closed their eyes again and regained the connection. Joe put his hand on Katie's stomach and said, "Concentrate on this area."

Katie concentrated on the area around her abdomen for several seconds before feeling it. She opened her eyes, let go of Joe's hand, and said, "Oh, my God. I felt another life."

"That's right," Joe said. "You're pregnant."

Katie cried with joy and hugged Joe. "I'm so happy. This is incredible. How many women get to connect with their baby like this?"

"I would guess you are the first in over a hundred years. That is the first time I have experienced it, too."

"This is the happiest day of my life," Katie said. "Except for our wedding day, of course."

Katie's phone rang, and she saw it was her former boss, Bob Martin. She answered it, put it on speakerphone, and said, "Hi, Bob. I'm here with Joe. How are you?"

"I'm okay. I hope you two had a nice honeymoon."

"We sure did," Joe said. "We spent a week in Katie's hometown. I got to know her family and friends and saw where she grew up."

"I wanted to go to Hawaii, but Joe thought snooping around my hometown would be more fun for some reason," Katie said.

"I'm sorry, but I'm afraid this isn't a social call," Bob said. "I have some terrible news."

Katie's happy face turned to concern as she looked at Joe. She looked back at the phone and said. "What's wrong? What happened?"

"Ashley's been shot. They don't expect her to survive."

Katie stood up in shock. She didn't know what to say. Joe stood up and put his arms around her as tears ran down her face.

"There's more," Bob continued. "Her mother was killed."

"Oh, my God," Katie finally said through the tears. "Where is she?"

"She's at Jackson McCormick Hospital."

"Okay, we're on our way. Thanks for letting us know."

Katie hung up the phone and said to Joe, "You can save her."

"Maybe," Joe said, "but we have to hurry."

Joe grabbed the suitcases he had brought inside and returned them to the car. Once they were on the road to Milwaukee, Joe used Katie's phone and called his grandson, Michael, to tell him what happened and that he would be away for a few more days.

Chapter 2

When they got on the highway, Katie drove extremely fast. Joe put his hand on her arm and said, "I understand you are concerned about your friend, but if we get into an accident, we won't be able to help her."

Katie looked at Joe and then at her speedometer, which read 95. She let up on the gas and slowed to 75. "I'm sorry, Joe. I'm just so worried we won't make it in time."

"I know you are, but there is only so much we can do right now. Your main concern should be getting us there safely and not getting pulled over by the police."

"You're right. I just don't want the day I learned about our baby to be a tragic day. I need you to tell me a story to distract me."

"A story? What kind of story?"

"I don't know. Just tell me something interesting from your past that you haven't told me before."

"Okay, let me think. Oh, I know. After the war ended, I went to California to shoot Yosemite National Park. I think it was 1946. Anyway, I ran into Ansel Adams in the hotel where I was staying."

"Ansel Adams? You mean the photographer?"

"The very one. So, you heard of him?"

"Of course. Who hasn't?"

"I don't know. As a photographer, I knew him because of his prominence in my field, but I wasn't aware he was popular with non-photographers."

"Well, Joe, just because you are older than my grandfather doesn't mean I can't teach you a thing or two."

"I have learned a lot since meeting you, Katie."

"Oh yeah? What have you learned?"

"I learned where your ticklish spots are," Joe said.

"Which I hate, by the way. What else did you learn?"

"I learned the most important lesson in my life."

Katie looked at him thoughtfully and said, "I assume you are talking about healing others."

5

"If it wasn't for you getting yourself blown up, I might never have figured it out."

"I'm so glad I could help," Katie said sarcastically. "It's not every day something good comes from getting blown up. Besides, you got yourself blown up, too."

"I would never recommend that, but it turned out well for us. I told you that fate would intervene and find a way to keep us together. That apartment exploding was the best thing that could have happened to us."

"It seems fate has a twisted sense of humor," Katie said.

"It worked out well for everyone except the MacKays. We ended up together, and David received money from both the insurance company and the developer, which enabled him to help his tenants settle into new apartments."

"And we are now married with a baby on the way. Don't forget about that," Katie said.

Katie started to cry. Joe put his hand on her arm and asked, "What's wrong?"

"This should be a happy day, and I want to be happy, but how can I, with Ashley in the hospital about to die? Don't answer that. Just finish your story about Ansel Adams."

"Okay, well, I was checking into my hotel and saw him walk by. A bellhop was helping him with his camera equipment. I recognized him and told him I was also a photographer. He was busy, but we arranged to meet later that evening to talk about photography."

"Bellhop? I haven't heard that word in a long time."

"Back then, he was a bellhop. Today, I guess you would call him a porter."

"If he's still around, I doubt he carries people's luggage."

"I'm glad you haven't lost your sense of humor. Anyway, we met that evening and had a great conversation. I learned a lot from him. He was a pioneer in the field and a really nice guy."

"That sounds like a good memory," Katie said as she looked at her gas gauge. "I'm not sure if we have enough gas to get there."

Joe glanced at the gauge and said, "Every car I ever had still had plenty of gas after the gauge said empty."

"That was years ago, Joe. I'm not sure it works that way anymore."

"It's up to you if you want to stop, but I think pushing on is worth the risk."

Katie decided Joe was right, and thirty minutes later, they pulled into the hospital parking lot with the gas gauge reading slightly below empty. "I'm so glad we didn't stop," Katie said as they exited the car.

***

They hurried inside and asked where they could find Ashley Taylor. The woman at the information desk directed them to room 406. They rushed to the elevator and waited. They waited some more. Katie looked at her watch. Why did the damn elevator have to be so slow at a time like this? Finally, it opened, and they got in. Katie pressed the button for the fourth floor and then pressed the close button several times before the door finally closed. It started moving up but stopped on the second floor. The doors opened, and a nurse got in. She hit the button for the third floor, and Katie sighed heavily, which got her a dirty look from the nurse.

They raced to find Ashley's room when the elevator door opened on the fourth floor. Her husband, John, stood outside the room with their two kids. The older child, a boy, was about ten years old, and the younger child, a girl, was about seven. A well-dressed middle-aged man of about fifty stood beside them while John signed something on a clipboard and handed it to the man.

Katie waited until he left, hugged John, and said, "We came as soon as we heard. How is she?"

John said softly, "The priest from Virginia's church is delivering the last rites. I didn't want the kids to see that. We hardly ever go to church anymore, which I regret now. Maybe this is punishment."

Katie held his hands and said, "You are not being punished. Don't think like that. You must have faith."

"I wish I could, Katie, but I need to face reality."

"It's not over yet. I believe she will recover."

"I like your optimism, Katie, but optimism won't help her now."

"It seems like a bad time to be bothering you with paperwork," Joe said.

"That was the hospital administrator. I gave him permission to donate Ashley's organs. I think she would want that."

The door opened, and the priest came out. He spoke to John while Joe and Katie slipped into the room. Ashley's father was sitting by her side, tears running down his face. Katie hugged him and said, "Don't worry, Henry. I am confident she will pull through."

"If I lose her, I don't think I could go on."

"You won't lose her. I promise."

"Ashley is lucky to have friends like you, Katie."

"Do you mind if we spend some time alone with her?"

Henry nodded and stood up. "Take all the time you need," he said before leaving the room.

Joe sat where Ashley's father had been sitting and put his hand on Ashley's hand. Katie sat in a chair on the other side and held her other hand. Joe concentrated for about fifteen seconds before saying, "She has extensive damage to her liver and one of her kidneys. It looks like the surgeons removed most of the bullet fragments, but some remain. They probably couldn't get to them without causing more harm."

"Can you fix the damage?" Katie asked.

"Yes, but it will take time. I'm not sure how long we can stay here before people start wondering what we're doing."

"You just get started, and we'll worry about that when it becomes a problem."

Joe started with the bullet fragments. He instructed Ashley's body to push them away to an area where they wouldn't be a problem. He then concentrated on repairing the damage. After ten minutes, the door opened, and John entered with the kids. Katie looked up and said, "We are praying."

"I did a lot of praying when they brought her in. Hopefully, it will work better for you."

"Maybe we should all pray together," Katie said, hoping to give Joe more time to work.

"That's a good idea," John said, motioning for his children to come closer. They held hands and were silent for about five minutes before the kids started to get antsy. Joe let go of Ashley's hand and said to Katie. "I think we should give the kids some time with their mom." He motioned for Katie to follow him, and they left the room.

When Katie closed the door, she said, "What happened in there?"

"I was able to get her out of danger, but there's more work to do. She will be okay for now."

Katie hugged Joe, kissed him, and said, "I love you so much. Do you think we can get something to eat now? I'm starving."

"You read my mind," Joe said.

Waiting for the elevator was again a painstakingly long process. When the doors finally opened, Gabe Garcia stepped out. "Katie. Joe. It's good to see you again," he said.

"It's good to see you, too, Gabe," Katie said. "I just wish it were under better circumstances."

"Me, too. How is Ashley?"

"She'll be fine," Joe said.

"Really? I was under the impression she was near death."

"Sometimes miracles happen," Joe said.

"I guess I shouldn't be surprised. I thought the same thing about you three months ago, and look at you now. I mean, who gets hit by a car and then blown up and comes out without a scratch?"

"I guess I'm lucky," Joe said.

"Seems more like divine intervention if you ask me."

"We were heading out to get some dinner," Katie said. "Would you like to join us?"

"Sure. I could go for a bite to eat right now. If you like German food, there's a great restaurant about two blocks from here."

"I know the place," Katie said. "We'll meet you there, but we have to stop for gas first."

***

Fifteen minutes later, they pulled into the parking lot of Das Bayerisches Haus. Gabe arrived before them, and Katie parked next to his car. When they went inside, a pretty young woman wearing a dirndl designed to show off plenty of cleavage led them to a table near the bar. She set menus in front of them and said, "Your server will be with you shortly."

Katie looked at Gabe and said, "I see why you like this place."

"Hey, I'm a happily married man."

"Sure, but a little eye candy never hurt anybody, right?"

"You said that, not me. I will deny it under interrogation."

9

They all laughed as their server came to their table. She was even prettier than the first girl. "Good evening. My name is Hannah. Can I get you started with a drink?"

"Bring us three Warsteiners, please," Gabe said. He looked at Katie and Joe and said, "I'm buying. You can't go to a German restaurant without getting a beer."

When the woman turned to leave, Katie put her hand in front of Joe's eyes and said, "Nothing to see here."

Joe laughed and said, "Please, you are the prettiest girl in the room."

"You two need to get a room," Gabe said.

"We do need to get a room," Joe said. "We left home in such a hurry that we didn't think about a hotel."

"Our oldest is away at college. You can use his room. I'm sure my wife wouldn't mind."

"That is very nice of you, Gabe," Katie said, "but we are newlyweds."

"Say no more," Gabe said. "There's a Hilton not too far from the hospital."

"Good idea," Katie said. "We want to be close to Ashley."

The server came back and set the beers on the table. After everyone ordered and she left, Gabe asked, "Do you really believe that Ashley will recover?"

"I know she will," Joe said.

"How do you know?"

"That is hard to explain, but take my word for it."

Gabe looked at him momentarily and said, "What does her husband believe?"

Katie interjected, saying, "John will be pleasantly surprised tomorrow morning."

"I hope you are right," Gabe said.

"By the way, Gabe, congratulations on your promotion to captain," Katie said. "Did you come to the hospital as a friend, or are you on the case?"

"Both," Gabe said. "I am investigating this personally."

"What have you learned so far?" Beth asked.

"Not much. Ashley went to visit her mother at work. Her mom works at Social Services. Someone shot them outside in the parking lot near Ashley's car."

"Are there cameras there?" Joe asked.

"Unfortunately, not in the parking lot. We got footage from a couple of cameras inside the building, but nothing useful was on them."

"Can you get us a copy?" Katie asked.

Gabe looked at her and said, "You're no longer an investigative reporter, Katie."

"Ashley is my friend. I want to help any way I can."

Gabe sighed and said, "I suppose nothing I say will change your mind, so I will only ask that you share any information you learn."

"Just like old times," Katie said.

After dinner, Gabe returned to the hospital to speak with John while Joe and Katie drove to the hotel.

They got a nice room on the fourth floor overlooking the city. After bringing their stuff to the room, Joe said, "It's getting late. We may be able to get some alone time with Ashley."

"I agree. Let's go."

***

Ashley's father, husband, and their kids were still there when Joe and Katie arrived at the hospital. When John saw them, he said, "You were right. The doctor said Ashley is stable. He said he's never seen anything like it. It's a miracle. I mean, she's not out of the woods yet, but there's hope now. Maybe I underestimated the power of prayer."

"It's getting late," Katie said. "You guys should go home and get some rest. We'll stay with Ashley for a while."

"That's probably a good idea," John said. "The kids are getting tired."

"Go," Katie said. "I'll call you if there is any change."

They exchanged numbers, and John left with Henry and the kids. Joe and Katie sat next to Ashley as before and held her hands. Joe concentrated on healing Ashley, and Katie sat quietly, thinking about all the good times she spent with her friend. After forty-five minutes, a nurse entered the room and said, "Visiting hours are over."

"Please," Katie said. "Give us a little more time."

The nurse looked at her watch and said, "Okay, I can pretend I didn't see you, but you need to be out in thirty minutes."

"Okay, we will be gone before then," Katie said. "Thank you."

After twenty-five minutes, Katie looked at her watch and said, "Okay, Joe. We need to leave."

Just then, Ashley's eyes opened. She took a deep breath, looked at Joe, and said, "Oh, my God!"

Joe let go of Ashley's hand, and she said, "I felt you. I felt me. I don't know what I felt."

Katie stood up, hugged her friend, and said, "It's all right, Ashley. It's nothing to worry about. I'm so happy you are okay."

Ashley looked around and said, "Where am I? What happened?" She then looked at Joe and said, "What are you?"

Joe looked at Katie, who said, "Joe has a special ability. He is a Healer."

"A Healer?" Ashley asked, confused.

"Yes. He has the ability to heal others. Do you remember when that apartment exploded, and Joe was hurt so much more than I was? The truth is, I was hurt even worse than he was, but he used his healing abilities on me instead of himself.

Ashley looked at Joe and said, "That's right. You went from near death to perfectly fine in less than a week."

"I could have recovered in a couple of days, but that would have drawn too much attention to me," Joe said.

"Also, when I hit him with my car, it was worse than I let on," Katie said. "I thought he might die, but he was fine later the next day."

"I thought it was strange that he broke your windshield and didn't get hurt."

"Now that you know, Ashley, I'd like you not to tell anyone," Joe said. "If word got out, my life would never be normal again."

She looked at Katie, who nodded. She looked back at Joe and said, "I'll keep your secret, but I don't understand any of this. Why am I in the hospital? What happened to me?"

The nurse returned to the room and noticed Ashley was awake. "Oh, my!" she said. "You're awake. How is this possible? You were given last rites just a few hours ago."

"It's a miracle," Katie said.

The nurse checked the monitor and said, "I'll get the doctor."

She left the room, and Ashley asked again, "What happened to me?"

Katie asked, "You don't remember?"

Ashley thought about it and said, "I remember going to see my mom. I remember parking the car. I don't remember anything after that."

Katie looked at Joe and back at Ashley. "I don't know if we should be the ones telling you this. Perhaps I should call your husband. He left with your dad to bring the kids home about an hour ago."

"Why can't you tell me? What the hell happened? Why am I in the hospital?"

"Well, I'm afraid I have terrible news." She looked back at Joe as if she hoped he could help her with the words and then said, "You and your mom were attacked. Someone shot both of you."

Ashley looked shocked and said, "What? Where is she? Where's Mom?"

There was an awkward moment of silence. Ashley shook her head and said, "No! It can't be true."

Katie held Ashley's hand and said, "I'm so sorry."

Ashley started crying as the door opened, and the doctor came in, followed by the nurse. He saw Ashley awake and said, "This is unbelievable." He walked to her bedside and said, "Mrs. Taylor, how do you feel?"

"I just learned my mother is dead. How the hell do you think I feel?"

He looked at Joe and Katie and then back at Ashley. "I'm so sorry," he said. "It was a tragedy, but we thought we lost both of you."

Ashley took a deep breath and said, "I'm sorry I snapped at you, Doctor. I know it's not your fault."

"That's quite all right. I think it is good to let your anger out at a time like this."

"What happened? Who shot us and why?"

"Nobody knows yet," Katie said, "but we're going to find out."

The doctor checked on Ashley. He checked her eyes and listened to her chest. He said, "I'm going to order a few tests. In the meantime, welcome back to the land of the living." He walked out with the nurse following. Nobody asked them to leave, so Katie and Joe sat down beside Ashley again.

"I think John needs to know you're awake," Katie said, taking out her phone. She dialed John's number and put it on speaker. John answered and said, "Hi, Katie. Is Ashley okay?"

"Maybe we should let her answer that," Katie said, holding her phone in front of Ashley.

"Hi, Honey."

"Ashley! Oh, my God! You're okay. I don't believe it. I was so worried."

"Do you know about Mom?"

"Yes. I'm so sorry, Honey. Listen, your dad is here. He'll watch the kids. I'm coming back there right now. We'll talk about everything when I get there."

After they hung up, Ashley asked Joe, "Can you show me that healing thing again?"

Joe looked at Katie, who nodded. "Okay, just for a little while."

Joe held her hand and concentrated. He felt Ashley from the inside like she was an extension of his body. He could feel her heart, lungs, and all her internal organs. Ashley could feel everything, too. She could even feel Joe's internal organs. "This is incredible," she said. "I've never felt anything like this."

"Don't talk, Ashley. Just feel. Feel what is right and what is wrong. Concentrate," Joe said.

They stayed silent for about a minute, and then Joe said, "Can you feel what needs fixing?"

"Yes. I think I do. I don't know how, but I can feel what's wrong."

"Now, we are going to direct your body to make repairs. Just feel. Don't talk."

They stayed like that for about fifteen minutes before Joe let go. "I think we should stop now. Your husband will be here soon. Remember, this is our secret."

"I don't think I can lie to my husband, Joe."

"I thought that might be a problem," Joe said. "You have to understand that I am different. Can you imagine what would happen to me if word got out about what I can do?"

Ashley thought for several seconds and said, "I'll tell him God sent an angel to heal me. That's not really a lie."

"I guess that will work, but I'm no angel."

"I'm not so sure. You are the closest thing to an angel I've ever seen."

"He's my angel," Katie said. "Get your own."

They both laughed, and Ashley started crying. Katie held her hand, and Ashley said, "I'm sorry. I was thinking about Mom. How can I laugh at a time like this?"

"I'm sure your mom would be happy you are okay and would not want to see you sad."

Ashley wiped tears from her eyes and said, "I suppose you're right."

"I felt the same way only a few hours ago. I received great news moments before learning what happened to you. I felt so guilty about being happy."

"What was your great news?" Ashley asked.

"I learned that I'm pregnant," Katie said.

"You're pregnant? That's fantastic news. Congratulations. You should be happy. Oh, and I ruined it for you. I'm so sorry."

"You didn't ruin anything. Don't be silly. This was certainly not your fault."

The door opened, and John walked in. He saw Ashley sitting up in bed and rushed to her side. They hugged for a long moment, and then John stood up and shook Joe's hand. He then went to Katie and hugged her. "I don't know how it is possible that Ashley is alive and well, but you knew. I don't know how you knew, but I can't help feeling that you two had something to do with it."

"That's crazy talk," Katie said. "We just happen to be optimistic."

John looked at Katie for a moment before turning back to Ashley. He held her hand and said, "Your dad and the kids will be so happy to see you."

"How is Dad handling this?"

"It's rough on him, but the burden of losing both a wife and a daughter has been lifted. I think your Mom's death and your near death had brought him to a dark place, but your miracle recovery has brought him out of it."

Joe interrupted and said, "I think this is a good time for Katie and me to leave. It's late, and we both need to get some sleep."

"Of course," John said, shaking Joe's hand again. "Thank you both for coming."

"Thank you for everything," Ashley said, stressing the word "everything."

John looked at her, puzzled, but said nothing.

When Joe and Katie returned to the hotel, they were exhausted. They got undressed and went straight to bed. As a newlywed couple, it was common for them to make love before going to sleep, but they were both too tired for that.

Chapter 3

Katie and Joe woke up later than usual the following morning. Before doing anything else, they took a shower together. They washed each other, and then Joe stood behind Katie and put his arms around her. Katie put her hands on his as he slid one hand down to her stomach and said, "Can you believe what we made together?"

Katie turned around and kissed Joe passionately. They made love in the shower. When they finished, they dried themselves, went to bed, and made love again.

They lay in bed for a while, and then Katie said, "I suppose we should get dressed and go back to the hospital. Do you think Ashley needs more healing?"

"I think she can survive without further treatments, but there is more that I can do. I would like to get her back to a hundred percent before we return home."

"It will be hard with people around," Katie said. "You will need to do it a little at a time when she is alone. That will give us time to investigate what happened to her."

"Do you think there is something we can do that the police can't do?"

"I don't know. We solved the last case without much help from the police."

"We got lucky. Plus, the police were hampered by their own captain."

"We worked hard, and I am proud of what we accomplished. Don't diminish what we did."

"I'm sorry, Katie. I remember you feeling like a failure, and I don't want you ever to feel that way again. I worry what will happen if you get your hopes up and we fail to find the killer."

"I was wrong to feel that way, and it won't happen this time. If we fail, I will at least know we tried."

Joe kissed Katie and said, "Okay, my love. It will be fun working on a case with you again."

They got up and got ready. After getting dressed, they went downstairs and had breakfast at the hotel restaurant. They then headed to the hospital.

Ashley's room was a full house. John and Henry were there with the kids. Bob Martin was also there. When he saw Katie, he hugged her and said, "It's so nice to see you again, Katie. It's a shame you had to end your honeymoon this way."

"At least Ashley is okay," Katie said.

"I'm very happy about that. It seems someone made a big mistake with her diagnosis."

"Yes, that must be what happened," Katie said.

"Well, I just came to check on Ashley. The room is getting a bit full, so I should probably return to work."

"Before you leave, I would like to talk to you," Katie said.

"Of course," Bob said before leaving the room, followed by Katie and Joe. Joe closed the door behind him, and Bob said, "What's up?"

"Well, someone shot Ashley and murdered her mother. Do you have an investigator working on the case?"

"Unfortunately, Katie, after you left, we've been having trouble finding an investigative reporter worth a damn. We moved Kevin into the role, but he couldn't cut it. Besides, it looks like it was a random mugging. Their purses were left behind, but their cash was taken. It's a rough area. It was probably a drug addict looking for money. It will be hard to find someone like that."

"That was exactly what they said about the last case, and we proved them wrong."

"This isn't your last case, Katie. Sometimes, bad people do bad things to random people."

"That very well may be the case, but I still want to look into it. Ashley deserves to know who killed her mother and why."

Bob looked at Katie, slowly nodded, and said, "Okay, what can I do?"

"If we find something, we may need Billy's help. Will you ask him to cooperate with us?"

"I can't do that, but I can hire you back temporarily. Your old desk is still empty. It's yours until you find the killer or give up looking. If you do find something, it will be your duty to report it for Channel 23 News."

She shook Bob's hand, "You've got yourself a deal." She hugged him and said, "Thank you so much."

Joe and Katie returned to Ashley's room. When John saw them come in, he said, "Ashley would like to spend some time with her friends, meaning you, of course, so we are going to head home for a while. I need to make lunch for the kids anyway. They stayed home from school today."

When everyone left, Katie sat on one side of Ashley, and Joe sat on the other. "Are you ready for more healing?" Joe asked.

"I sure am," she said.

"Wait," Katie said. "Before we start, let's go over what happened yesterday. Why were you visiting your mother on a weekday during working hours?"

Ashley thought for a moment and said, "I think she asked me to see her, but I don't remember why. Wait! I do remember. She wanted to show me something. She thought our news station would be interested in it."

"What was it?" Katie asked.

"Ashley thought for a long while and finally said, "I'm sorry. I can't remember."

"It's okay," Joe said. "It might come to you. We should probably start now while nobody is here."

"Good idea," Ashley said. "Let's do this."

They held hands, and Joe connected with Ashley again. He worked to repair the damage he had not been able to fix the last time. After about thirty minutes, Ashley sat up and screamed.

Katie stood up and grabbed her arms. "What is it? What happened?"

"I saw something. A man in a ski mask. He shot Mom."

"Is this a memory?" Katie asked.

"Yes. I think so. I remember him shooting Mom twice and then turning the gun on me."

Katie looked at Joe, who said, "She had a little swelling in her brain. It was probably from falling and hitting her head on the pavement. It's possible some of her memories returned when the swelling went down."

"What was the man in the mask wearing?" Katie asked.

Ashley thought briefly, saying, "He was wearing a blue ski mask and a black jacket. A leather jacket, I think. Yes, a leather jacket."

"That's good. Do you remember anything else?" Katie asked.

"Yes. I remember meeting Mom in her office. I remember she took a folder from her top drawer and handed it to me."

"What was in the folder?" Katie asked.

Ashley thought very hard and finally shook her head. "I don't remember. I can see the folder in my mind, but can't see what's in it."

"It's okay," Katie said. "I think we've put you through enough for now. We'll come back later and check on you."

Ashley grabbed Katie's hand and reached out to take Joe's hand. "You two have been a godsend. I don't think I could ever repay you for what you've done."

"Seeing you alive and well is more than payment enough," Katie said.

Ashley reached out her hands, inviting them for a group hug. They said their goodbyes and left. When they got to Katie's car, Joe asked, "What do you want to do now?"

"Let's go to the scene of the crime."

***

Joe and Katie headed to the Social Services building where Victoria Hall worked. On the way, Katie said, "It feels great that we were able to help Ashley. I should say you were able to help Ashley."

"We are a team, Katie."

"Yes, but you are the Healer."

"If it weren't for you doing the research, I would have never known I had the ability to heal anyone but myself, and if you weren't near death after that explosion, I would not have learned how to do it."

"I guess you're right," Katie said. "We are a good team."

"We sure are, and to answer your question, helping Ashley was a fantastic feeling. I want to help other people, too, but there is no way I can do that without them learning my secret."

"Yes, that is a problem. Maybe there is a way around it."

"Oh, yeah? How would that work?"

"I have no idea. Maybe we can talk to Mrs. Babic while we are in town. She might know something."

"That's a great idea, Katie. Even if she can't help, it would be nice to see her again."

"Yes. She's a nice lady."

When they reached the social services building, they parked on the street in front of the entrance. They walked past several people hanging around the front door and went inside. Katie said to a woman behind the counter, "Hi. My name is Katie, and this is Joe. We're from Channel 23 News. We're investigating the murder of Victoria Hall."

"Oh, yes. We are all very saddened by what happened."

"Do you know if there were any witnesses?" Katie asked.

"I don't think so, but I only work part-time and wasn't here when it happened. Let me get you someone who might know more than me." She picked up her phone, dialed a number, and said, "Hi, Holly. Could you please come out to the lobby? There are a couple of reporters here asking about Victoria."

Twenty seconds later, a woman approached the lobby. She was in her mid-thirties with dark, curly hair and glasses that Joe thought looked like a style women wore back in the sixties. He figured the style came back around. Either that or the woman was wearing her grandmother's glasses. "Hi. I'm Holly Johnson," she said and held out her hand.

They shook hands, and Katie said, "I'm Katie, and this is Joe. We are from Channel 23 News. First, we would like to express our condolences for your loss. I knew Victoria personally, so I know how you feel."

"You did? How did you know her?"

"I'm friends with her daughter, Ashley."

"Oh, that's right. I remember Victoria telling me about her daughter's career at the television station. She was very proud of her."

"Were you here when her daughter came to visit her?" Joe asked.

"Yes. I was in my office, next to Victoria's office, but I must have been busy because I didn't notice anything until I heard a commotion in the hallway. Someone was yelling that they heard gunshots in the parking lot. People were initially afraid to go outside, but slowly, they started venturing out to see what happened. I believe it was Mark who found the bodies. I mean, he found Victoria and Ashley."

"Who's Mark?" Katie asked.

"Mark Jones. He's our IT guy."

"Can we speak with him?" Katie asked.

"Sure. Follow me."

She led them down a hallway and turned right. They went to the end of that hallway, and Holly knocked on the door to the right before opening it. A young man sat behind a desk that held three computer monitors. He was young with straight, dark hair that was somewhat messy. Joe thought he looked similar to Billy, the computer nerd at Katie's office.

"Mark," Holly said. "This is Katie and Joe. They are from the news station. They want to talk to you about Victoria."

He stood up and shook their hands. "What's there to talk about? Somebody shot her, and now she's dead. I just happened to find her first. I didn't see it happen."

"Where were you when you heard the shots?" Joe asked.

"I was in the hallway near the back door. I just finished doing a software upgrade on the computer in the meeting room."

"How many shots did you hear?" Katie asked.

"Three. It was bang, bang, then a pause, then another bang."

Did you go outside right away?" Katie asked.

"No. I yelled that I heard gunshots. I then yelled for someone to call 911. I looked out the back door to see if I could see the shooter, but saw no one. By then, several people were looking out the door with me. After a minute or so, I decided the person was probably gone, so I went outside. A few other people came out behind me."

"Please don't take this the wrong way," Joe said. "It just seems unusual that a computer nerd would be the first one out the door in a dangerous situation."

Katie looked at Joe. She would have been surprised three months ago, but she now knew Joe was not the best at being diplomatic.

"I'm not a nerd. I'm a geek, and I know a little about guns. That was the sound of a 9-millimeter pistol. It's a great weapon at close range, but you couldn't hit a barn door with it at a hundred feet. That's an exaggeration, but the point is, I wasn't too worried."

"Since you know about guns, how do we know you didn't shoot them and then run inside and sound the alarm?" Joe asked.

"Because several people rushed out into the hallway as soon as they heard the shots. Also, I found Victoria and her daughter at least forty yards from the back door, maybe more. There would be no way I could get back inside so quickly if I were the shooter."

"Will you show us where you found them?" Katie asked.

"Sure. Follow me," Mark said and led the group outside. They walked past several cars until they reached an area marked off by police tape. "It happened right here. There was a car here at the time. Victoria was lying on the ground on the passenger side, and her daughter was on the driver's side."

Joe looked around. There were several vans in the parking lot, including two nearby. They would have made good cover for an attacker. "Do most of these vehicles here belong to employees?" Joe asked.

"Yes," Holly said. "I would guess over ninety percent of them."

"Is there assigned parking?"

"No, but people usually park in the same place. Why?"

"I just want to know what this parking lot looked like at the time of the murder. Mark, did you notice if these two vans were here yesterday?"

Mark thought for a moment and said, "Yes. I believe they were."

"Do you think someone hid behind one of these vans and ambushed them?" Katie asked.

"Perhaps," Joe said. "Or maybe they used them to disappear after the shooting. Either way, it looks easy for a person to go unnoticed in this parking lot."

"Can either of you think of a reason someone would want to shoot Victoria?"

"She was a nice lady," Mark said. "I don't know anyone who didn't like her."

"I agree," said Holly. "It couldn't have been anyone who works here, and I doubt any of her clients would want to hurt her."

"Her door says, 'Senior Case Worker.' Does that mean she was like a supervisor, or did she have her own clients?" Katie asked.

"She had her own people that she worked with, but she also helped other case workers when they needed help," Holly said.

"Did she ever talk to you about problem clients?" Katie asked.

"Sure. Often, she would talk about an issue she had in the past if it was similar to a problem I was facing at the time."

"What about anything recently?"

"If she was having a problem with someone recently, she didn't mention it to me, although one of her clients did die recently. It was an overdose, I think."

"Really," Joe said. "Who was that?"

"I'm afraid we can't give out personal information about our clients."

"But he's dead," Joe said. "Who's going to care?"

"I'm sorry," Holly repeated. "My hands are tied."

"Well, thank you both for your time," Katie said. She was about to hand her a business card, but remembered that after she quit, she no longer needed the cards, so she threw them away. Now, she wished she had kept a few.

They followed Holly back through the building. Joe looked up, searching for cameras, but only saw two in the lobby. Katie thanked Holly again before she and Joe left.

"When they returned to the car, Katie said, "I think we should talk to Gabe."

**

"We're here to see Captain Garcia," Katie said after they arrived at the police station.

The police officer behind the counter was big. He was several inches taller than Joe and quite muscular. He did not look like someone who belonged behind a counter. Joe wondered what he had done wrong to get assigned the receptionist job. "The captain is very busy," the officer said. "Is there something I can help you with?"

"I'm afraid not. It's about the Victoria Hall murder. Please let him know Katie and Joe Novak are here."

The officer picked up his phone and dialed an extension number. After several seconds, he said, "Hi, Captain. There's a Kathy and Joe Novak here to see you."

"Katie," Katie said.

"Sorry. There's a Katie and Joe Novak here to see you. What should I tell them?"

After several more seconds, he hung up the phone and said, "Follow me."

He led them past several desks until they reached the captain's office. "Go right in. He's expecting you."

Katie opened the door and said, "Hi, Gabe."

They both walked into the office, and Joe said. "Wow, Gabe," This is much nicer than your last office."

"You mean my cubicle without the cube?"

"That's the one."

"My wife likes it too. She visits me for lunch sometimes, and now we can close the door."

Joe looked at all the glass windows and said, "I think you need curtains for that."

"That's not what we do in here," Gabe said. "She just likes the privacy. Of course, a nice office isn't free. A lot of extra work came with these four walls."

"I'm sure you can handle it, Gabe," Katie said.

"Every day is a challenge," he said, and motioned for them to have a seat.

"So, what did that big guy do to end up behind a desk?" Joe asked.

"Arnold? He didn't do anything wrong if that's what you mean. Everyone takes turns filling in when needed."

"Arnold?" Katie said. "Is that really his name?"

"No. His real name is George, but people around here have started calling him Arnold for obvious reasons, and the name is stuck. I assume you two have started your investigation. Is that why you're here?"

"Yes," Katie said. "I'm officially working for Channel 23 News again."

"Wow! You got your old job back? What about the resort?"

"It's just temporary. If we find anything, the station will get the story. In exchange, we will be able to use the station's resources."

"So, how can I help you?"

"You said you have videos from Victoria's office. Can we see them?" Joe asked.

"Sure," Gabe said, "But there is nothing useful on them." He opened a folder on his computer, found one of the video files, and double-clicked it to start playing. He turned the screen around and walked around the desk so he could watch it with Katie and Joe. "This is the lobby looking at the front door. It starts about a minute before Ashley arrives and ends a couple of minutes after she leaves."

He let the video run and, when it was over, said, "Unless you see something I don't, there is nothing useful on it."

"I don't see anything useful," Katie said. "Do you, Joe?"

Joe shook his head and said, "I saw two cameras in the lobby. Were there any others?"

"No. Just those two. So you saw the office this morning? Did you learn anything?"

"The man who found the body said the shots he heard were from a 9-millimeter pistol. Is that correct?" Katie asked.

"That's right," Gabe said.

"Is it hard to know that just by listening?"

"You would have to spend a lot of time on the gun range to get used to the different sounds. Honestly, I probably couldn't distinguish between a 9-millimeter and a .357. He could have also guessed. A 9-millimeter pistol is a common weapon these days."

"What about the second video?" Joe asked.

"Oh, yes," Gabe said before walking around his desk to start it.

The angle of this video showed the lobby with the door to Victoria's office in the background. They watched for about a minute before seeing Ashley walk to Victoria's office, open the door, and enter. The door closed behind her and remained closed for about four minutes. When it opened, Ashley and Victoria came out and disappeared off the right side of the screen.

Joe thought he saw something interesting but decided it wasn't worth mentioning, so he just asked, "Can we get a copy of that?"

"Sure," Gabe said, pulling a thumb drive from his desk. He copied the video onto it and handed it to Joe.

"Thank you," Joe said before handing the memory card to Katie.

"There is one other thing," Katie said. "Ashley remembered why she was at her mother's office. She said her mom called her and said she had a potential news story for the station."

Gabe looked surprised and said, "Really? Perhaps you should have started with that."

"Sorry. We asked what she was working on, but the client's files are confidential. Do you think you can get a subpoena or warrant or whatever you call it and find out what she was working on?"

"I'll try," Gabe said, "But I need to get a statement from Ashley before a judge will sign off on it. I'll head to the hospital after lunch and talk to her."

"Okay, Gabe. We appreciate any help you can give us."

"I consider you two friends. It's my pleasure to help you. I also want to find the person who killed Ashley's mother just as much as you do."

"You have Katie's number. Give us a call if you learn anything," Joe said.

"I will," Gabe said.

Chapter 4

As Katie and Joe were leaving the police station, Katie said, "We should get you a phone, Joe."

"No, thank you. I don't need the trouble."

"What do you mean by trouble?" Katie asked as they got into the car.

Joe put his seatbelt on and said, "I see people all the time connected to these new-fangled phones like smokers connected to cigarettes. It's an addiction I want no part of.

Katie started the car and backed out of the parking lot. She said when they were on the road, "If we didn't have a phone, it would be much harder to get the information we need."

"I agree, and you should have a phone, but we don't need two phones."

"I'm pregnant now, Joe. What if the baby has a problem, and I need to contact you?"

"I won't let that happen. Besides, we are almost always together."

"Okay, Joe," Katie said as she put her hand on his. "Part of me is glad you don't want a phone. The old-fashioned side of you is quite a turn-on."

They kissed, and it soon became passionate. Katie pulled away and said, "No! We almost drove off the road the last time we did that."

"Where are we going, by the way?" Joe asked.

"It's almost lunchtime. I thought we could stop and get something to eat."

"You're eating for two, now. We should find something healthy."

"What would you suggest?" Katie asked.

"I don't know. Let's see what you need. Pull over up here."

There was a bank ahead, and Katie parked in a spot as far from other cars as she could find. They held hands, and Joe concentrated. He always knew what his own body needed for nutrients, and now he could feel what Katie needed, too. After thirty seconds, he let go and said, "I think we can both benefit from some leafy green vegetables, like a salad."

"I know a good place nearby," Katie said before backing out of the parking space and getting back on the road. They drove for five minutes before parking in front of a Greek restaurant. It was a small place between a barber shop and a cell phone store. "I thought we could get Greek salads," Katie said.

"Good choice," Joe said as they got out of the car.

As they walked toward the door, Katie pointed at the cell phone store and asked, "Are you sure you don't want a phone? We can get a cheap flip phone without all the bells and whistles."

"Are you kidding? That's what they call a gateway drug."

"Look at you knowing something current."

"First, just because I don't watch television doesn't mean I don't know what is going on in the world. Second, the term 'gateway drug' has been around since long before you were born."

"Really? I didn't know that."

"It's true. Back in the seventies, people thought marijuana was a gateway drug. Now it's cheap cell phones."

Katie slapped Joe on the arm and said, "Come on. Let's eat."

They went inside and were seated by a pleasant, older woman who put menus in front of them and took their drink order. When she left, Joe asked, "What do you want to do after lunch?"

"I thought we could go see Mrs. Babic."

"I was hoping you would say that," Joe said.

"If you wanted to see her now, why didn't you just say so?"

"I don't know. I guess I like it when we think alike."

After lunch, Katie called Mrs. Babic, who was happy they wanted to come by. When they arrived, she greeted them at the door and said, "Come in. It's good to see you two again."

They all sat in the living room, and Joe said, "We were happy that you could come to our wedding."

"Oh, it was a beautiful ceremony, and I loved that resort of yours. It's so beautiful up there."

"Thank you," Joe said. "It is a nice reprieve from the city."

"So, what brings you to Milwaukee? I thought you two would be back to work after your honeymoon."

"We just got home when we learned someone had shot a good friend of mine," Katie said.

"Oh, my! Is she okay?"

"She is now. Joe saved her life, but, unfortunately, her mother was killed."

Mrs. Babic, who was sitting on a chair next to Katie, leaned over, put her hand on Katie's, and said. "That's terrible. I'm so sorry."

"At least we made it here in time to save my friend," Katie said.

"I'm so glad you discovered how to use your ability to help others," Mrs. Babic said. "I know that was important to you."

"That is one of the reasons we wanted to see you today," Joe said. "I'm not sure I am doing it right."

"Really? You saved a woman's life. How can you be doing it wrong?"

"He saved my life, too," Katie added.

"Oh, you saved the lives of two women. What can be wrong with that?"

"Well, when I connect with someone to heal them, they also connect to me. I can feel them as if they are a part of me, but they can feel what I feel. That means I can't help someone without them knowing my secret."

"Oh, that is a problem. So you're saying the person you are in contact with can feel everything you feel?"

"That's right. When I helped Katie's friend, she learned more about me than I wanted to give away. I'm lucky she is willing to keep my secret, but sooner or later, someone I help won't be so nice."

"I see your problem. It must also be a bit disconcerting for the people you help."

"It's an incredible feeling," Katie said. "When Joe saved me after that explosion, I thought I had died and was in heaven. I mean, I felt the pain, but there was this comforting feeling that I wasn't alone. Joe and I were connected in a way that is hard to imagine."

"That is something my grandmother never mentioned to me. She had experienced the Healer's touch several times. I would think if she felt what you are describing, she would have mentioned that."

"Really? So maybe I am doing something wrong."

"It's possible there is a better way to connect with people, but I don't know what you could do differently. Maybe you could consciously make it a one-way connection."

"How would I do that?"

"I don't know. Practice, I guess. Try it on me. Connect to me and then try to block me out."

Joe switched places with Katie on the sofa and held Mrs. Babic's hand. He connected with her, and she said, "Oh, wow! This is amazing. I understand now what you mean, Katie."

"Shhh," Joe said. "Give me a few minutes to concentrate."

"Everyone was quiet for a couple of minutes until Joe spoke. "Okay, now I'm going to try to block you."

Everyone was silent again. After five minutes, Mrs. Babic said, "I still feel you, Joe."

Joe opened his eyes and let go. "I have no idea how to block you."

"I felt what you did," Mrs. Babic said. "You focused most of your attention on a single part of me, but you also maintained a connection with the whole. Try focusing all your attention on one thing at a time. Try to avoid any connection to the brain, mine, and yours."

"I'll try," Joe said, "but a hundred years of conditioning may be hard to erase."

Mrs. Babic held out her hand and said, "Just try."

Joe held her hand and connected with her again. After several minutes, he let go and said, "Did you feel anything different?"

"I think it worked," she said. "Twice, for a few seconds each, I felt alone. You need lots of practice, but you should be able to help people without them knowing it."

Joe got up and hugged her, "Thank you so much, Mrs. Babic. You've been a great help."

"Please, call me Katarina. After all, you are my older cousin. Besides, there's no need to thank me. You helped me even more than I helped you."

They said their goodbyes, and when they returned to the car, Katie asked, "What did she mean when she said you helped her more?"

"She had a small tumor growing in her left breast. It shouldn't be a problem for her anymore."

Katie leaned over and kissed Joe. "I don't think any wife has ever been prouder of her husband than I am right now."

***

Katie and Joe decided to check on Ashley. When they arrived at her room, Gabe Garcia was already there. They greeted each other, and Katie said, "Have you got Ashley's statement yet?"

"Yes, I did. She's been a big help."

"I still can't remember what Mom wanted me to know," Ashley said.

"It will come in time," Joe said.

"Well, I need to get back to work," Gabe said. He handed Ashley a business card and said, "Please call me if you remember anything else."

After he left, Katie said, "Where are John and your father?"

"We decided that since I am feeling better, John should return to work, and the kids should be in school. Dad is arranging Mom's funeral. I wish I could be with him right now."

Katie held Ashley's hand and said, "I'm sure he knows that. You've taken an enormous burden off his plate just by getting better."

"But now that I am better, I should be out there helping him."

"You're not better," Joe said. "I mean, you are better, but you are not better enough. You still have bullet fragments inside you, and the last time I checked, there was still a little swelling around the brain. Let's work on the swelling today. We can push out the bullet fragments, but that would make a mess that would be difficult to explain. We should wait until you get home for that. We also don't want to fix the scarring until after you leave here."

"When do you think I can get out of here?"

"Let's do a healing session first. I will know more when we're done."

Joe sat next to Ashley and held her hand. He said, "I'm going to try something new. I'm going to try to feel you without you feeling me."

"What? Why would you do that? Feeling that connection and knowing what is going on inside of me is just so incredible."

"I know it is, Ashley, but I need to practice this. I want to be able to help others without giving away my secret."

"Okay," Ashley said reluctantly. "You can practice on me. If I can help you to help other people, that would also be an amazing feeling. Not equally amazing, but still up there."

Joe smiled and said, "Okay. Here we go."

He formed a connection with Ashley and tried hard to concentrate solely on her injuries. He found it hard to reduce the swelling around her brain without concentrating on the brain itself. After nearly twenty minutes, the door opened, and Ashley's doctor came in. "How are you feeling today, Mrs. Taylor?"

"I feel fine," she said. "When can I go home?"

The doctor looked at her chart and said, "People around here are calling you 'The Miracle Woman.'" You were given last rites yesterday, and today, you are ready to go home. If this were the Middle Ages, people would have thought you were a witch."

"You called her a miracle woman," Katie said. "That implies an act of God, not the devil."

"I merely repeated what people are saying. I am a man of science," the doctor said. "I need to examine you, Mrs. Taylor. Would you like your guests to leave until we are finished?"

"No. I want them to stay."

"Very well," he said before taking out his stethoscope and listening to Ashley's chest. He pressed on Ashley's stomach and asked, "Does that hurt?"

"No. Not at all," Ashley said.

He moved his fingers over a few inches and pressed again. "What about now?"

"No. I don't feel any pain," Ashley said.

He looked at her chart again and said, "There's no indication on your chart that you were given any medication today. Is that correct?"

"That's right. Nobody gave me anything."

"So, what does your science tell you now?" Joe asked.

"I'm sure there is a logical reason why her health has improved so quickly, but I am stumped as to why that is."

"So what about sending me home? When can I leave?"

"I'm going to order a few more tests. I don't understand what happened to you, and I don't want to send you home until I am certain I haven't missed something. Let's give it one more night, and we'll revisit the question in the morning."

"Okay, Doctor. Thank you," Ashley said.

The doctor walked to the door, turned, and said, "I'll admit that I wish I could take credit for you getting better, but I say this truthfully that whatever, or even whoever, caused this amazing recovery, I am very happy for you, and I am also very sorry for the loss of your mother."

"I appreciate that, Doctor," Ashley said as he left the room.

When the door closed, Joe said, "Okay, tell me. What did you feel?"

"Well, I could tell you were struggling at the beginning. I could feel you off and on for a while. Gradually, the times I couldn't feel you got longer and longer. You still need practice, but you'll get there."

"Thanks for letting me use you as a guinea pig, Ashley."

"No. Not a guinea pig. I was more like a sparring partner."

"That's exactly right. If I want to get better, I need a sparring partner." He looked at Katie and said, "I need a couple of sparring partners."

Katie smiled and asked, "What do you think about her condition?"

"I think she's ready to go home now, but we've already drawn too much attention to her. Staying here another day wouldn't hurt."

"I don't mind playing sick for you, Joe, but I need to be out of here before Mom's funeral."

"I understand," Joe said. "I suspect the doctor will release you tomorrow."

The door opened, and Ashley's father came in. He hugged Ashley and said, "I can't believe it. You look so good. I always thought you were my miracle child, and now I know it."

"I always thought you were my miracle dad, too," Asley said.

Her dad hugged Katie and shook Joe's hand. "Thank you both for everything you have done," he said.

"We didn't do anything," Katie said.

He looked at Katie momentarily and said, "I don't know if Ashley's healing was a result of pure luck, a miracle from God, or something in the middle. I just can't shake this feeling that you two were involved somehow. I know that sounds crazy, but don't worry. I won't mention it to anyone else."

Katie smiled and said, "I think it's time for Joe and me to get going." She turned to Ashley and said, "We'll come by and check on you in the morning."

When they returned to Katie's car, Joe asked, "So, what do you want to do now?"

We're going back to the hotel.

"The hotel? It's still early."

"Watching you help others today has not only made me very proud, but it has also put me in a mood. When we get back to our room, you are going to make love to me until I tell you to stop, and then you are going to do it some more."

"Now that's an order I can't refuse."

Chapter 5

The following morning, after getting ready, Katie and Joe had breakfast in the hotel restaurant. As usual, Joe had a glass of orange juice while Katie sipped her coffee. "We should probably see Ashley before doing anything else," Katie said.

"I agree. The doctor may release her this morning."

They headed to the hospital after breakfast. Ashley's room was full of people when they arrived, like the first time they had been there. Unlike the first time, everyone had a smile on their face. Ashley's father stood on one side of her while John and the kids stood on the other.

"What's going on?" Katie asked.

"Ashley's being released today," John said.

"That's great news," Katie said. "What time?"

"He said it would take about two hours." He looked at his watch and added, "He said that about a half-hour ago, so she should be out of here around ten."

Katie walked over and hugged Ashley. "I'm so happy you are okay and will be leaving this place, " she said.

"Me too," Ashley said. "It's kind of depressing here."

"I hope you're not going home wearing that," Katie said, pointing at her hospital gown.

Ashley looked down and said, "Oh, hell no. John brought me a change of clothes. I just haven't had a chance to put them on yet."

"Now is probably a good time," Katie said.

"I agree, "Ashley said before turning to John. "Can you hand me my clothes, Honey?"

"Of course, Dear," John said before picking a bag off the floor and handing it to Ashley.

She got off the bed and carried the bag to the washroom. While she was getting dressed, Katie's phone rang. It was Bob Martin. "Good morning, Bob. Did you hear Ashley is leaving this morning?"

"I did. That's why I'm calling. I'm sending a photographer over there, and I want you to do the story."

"Me? I can't do that. I'm not prepared. I'm not dressed for television."

"Good. It will be more natural. You're Ashley's friend. Report it as a friend would report it."

"Okay. I'm in as long as Ashley will go along with it."

"A young man named Andrew is heading your way. He's new at the job, so cut him some slack."

"I hope he knows how to use a camera," Katie said.

"He's capable, or I wouldn't have hired him."

Ashley emerged from the bathroom just as Katie hung up the phone. She was wearing blue jeans, tennis shoes, and a pink sweater. Holding her arms up, she said, "I wouldn't have picked this outfit."

"What's wrong with it? I think you look great," Katie said.

"You're my friend. Of course, you would say that."

"Bob Martin called and wants me to cover your release."

"What? You want to film me dressed like this?"

"How do you think I feel?" Katie said. I'm dressed just like you, except my sweater is red. If anyone should be dressed nicely, it would be the reporter, not the person leaving the hospital."

"You have a point, Katie. Now I don't feel so bad."

"That's great. Now I do."

Joe, who had been listening quietly, decided to speak up, "I think you both look fantastic. No man watching is even going to notice what you are wearing."

Ashley looked at Katie and then back at Joe. "What about the women?"

Joe shook his head and said, "I give up."

Henry put his hand on Joe's shoulder and said, "You can live to be a hundred and still not understand women."

Joe smiled and said, "I'm certain you're right about that."

The door opened, and a young man carrying a video camera stepped in. The door started to close, hitting the camera and startling the young man, who turned and backed away from the door, stepping on Joe's foot.

He turned around and said, "Oh, I'm so sorry."

"It's okay. It'll heal," Joe said.

Katie stepped forward, put out her hand, and said, "You must be Andrew. I'm Katie."

He shook Katie's hand and said, "You can call me Andy. I'm pleased to meet you, Miss Katie."

"Mrs. I was married recently."

"Oh, Congratulations, Mrs. Katie. I know you by reputation. People at the station talk highly of you. I heard you caught a murderer on your very first investigation."

Katie put her hand on Joe's arm and said, "We caught a murderer. This is my husband, Joe Novak."

They shook hands, and Andy said, "I heard about you, too. You both got caught in an explosion and survived. Well, obviously."

"Yes. We were pretty lucky," Joe said.

"Just as lucky as Miss Ashley here, it seems."

"Mrs.," Ashley corrected.

"Mrs. I'm sorry. I keep getting that wrong."

"How long have you been with the station?" Katie asked.

"I started yesterday. This is my first assignment."

"Wonderful," Katie said.

"Don't worry, Miss, I mean Mrs. Katie. I do know what I'm doing. I used the same camera in school and know it inside and out."

"You know the camera, but what about everything else? What about lighting? Do you know when to shoot close and when to go wide? Will you notice if something in the background is sticking out of my head?"

"I'm sure he'll be fine, Katie," Joe said. "I'll work with him. If I notice something off, I'll mention it."

"Of course, you'll be fine, Andy. I'm sorry. I'm just used to Ashley behind the camera. Joe is an experienced photographer. He can help you if you need it."

"That's all right, Mrs. Katie. No need to apologize. I know I'm inexperienced, and I welcome any advice from you or Mr. Joe."

"Just Joe," Joe said.

"Okay, Joe. Where do you want to film?"

Joe looked at Katie and asked, "Do you want to film in here or outside?"

"I think we should film outside by the exit. I can talk to Ashley, and then Andy can film her getting in the car and driving away."

"That's a good idea, Mrs. Katie."

"Please, just Katie."

"Okay, Katie."

"Why don't we go downstairs and set up, Andy?" Joe said. "We can test the lighting and find the best spot to shoot from."

"Thanks, Joe," Katie said. "We'll be down as soon as Ashley is released."

After Joe and Andy left, Ashley said, "Hey, guys! Can you give Katie and me a few minutes? We have some girl stuff to talk about."

"Girl stuff?" John said. "Are you feeling okay?"

"It's girl stuff," Ashley repeated.

"Oh! Oh! Okay. We're leaving."

"After everyone left, Katie asked, "What's going on?"

"I remembered something else," Ashley said. "The paper my mom showed me had something to do with the deaths of homeless people."

"Really? How did they die? What's the connection to your mom?"

"I'm sorry. I don't know. That's all I remember."

"That's okay. This is the first real lead that we have so far."

"I just want you to find that son of a bitch that killed my mother."

Katie nodded, put her hand on Ashley's, and said, "We'll do our best."

"Thank you for everything, Katie."

Katie smiled and said, "I'm going to wait for you downstairs with Joe."

Katie opened the door and motioned for everyone to come back in. She then got on the elevator and headed down to the lobby.

Twenty minutes later, a nurse entered Ashley's room with a wheelchair. "Are you ready to leave this place?" she asked.

"I was ready yesterday, and I don't need that thing. I can walk out of here."

"I'm afraid it's hospital policy. Once you're outside, you can do what you want." She handed Ashley a clipboard and said, "I just need you to sign a few things, and then you can go home."

Ashley signed the papers and got into the chair. The nurse pushed her out of the room, followed by her father, husband, and kids. They all got in the elevator and headed downstairs. When they exited the elevator, over two dozen hospital employees lined both sides of the walkway. As Ashley passed, they all started clapping. Andy filmed the scene while Joe and Katie stood behind him, clapping. Ashley smiled and waved at everyone. When she got outside, she stood up while Katie moved beside her with a microphone.

"Hello, Milwaukee. This is Katie Novak here with Ashley Tayler. Ashley is my good friend and a beloved colleague to everyone at Channel 23 News. Two days ago, Ashley was shot while visiting her mom, Virginia Hall. Tragically, Ashley lost her mom that day. Virginia was a woman who dedicated her life to helping others. I knew her personally, and her loss... her loss has left a hole in my heart as I'm sure it has for many who knew her. Ashley herself was not expected to survive, but now, two days later, she is ready to go home. Ashley, would you like to say something to the people of Milwaukee?"

"I want to thank you first, Katie, and your husband, Joe. You two just returned from your honeymoon and then raced here to see me. You're true friends. I also want to thank everyone who has supported my family during this trying time."

"People at the hospital are calling you the miracle woman. Can you explain your miraculous recovery?"

"I'm certain that God sent an angel here to heal me."

"That is the best explanation that I have heard today. Thank you for your time, Ashley, and we look forward to your return to work. This is Katie Novak with Channel 23 News."

Andy continued to film while Ashley got in the car and drove away. Katie handed the microphone to Andy and said, "Good job, Andy. I think you have a future in this business."

***

On the way to Katie's car, Joe said. "Let's go back to the hotel. I want to look at that recording Gabe gave us again."

"Okay. What's on there you want to see?"

"I thought I saw something that wasn't quite right. It seemed minor when I first saw it, but I realized it may be important after thinking about it. I want to confirm my suspicion."

When they returned to the hotel, Katie opened her laptop and inserted the thumb drive into the slot. Katie opened the first video, but it was the wrong one. Joe said, "That's not it. Open the other one."

Katie opened the other video, and they watched Ashley enter her mom's office. They continued watching for a couple of minutes before Joe saw it. "Look. See the door next to Virginia's?"

"Barely," Katie replied.

"It just opened a crack. Keep watching."

They watched as Ashley and Virginia left the office and disappeared off the screen. A few seconds later, they saw the door to the right open all the way. They could only see about six inches of the door on the hinge side and couldn't see who had left the room. Katie backed up the video and stopped it. They could see part of a person's arm. "Is that Holly's office?" Katie asked.

"It must be. She said her office is next to Virginia's, and there isn't an office on the other side."

"She's wearing something black, although there's not much detail in the video. I can't tell if it's a leather jacket or just a black shirt."

"We should pay her another visit," Joe said.

"I agree. I think this is a good time to do a Channel 23 News interview. I know your camera is still in the suitcase, but did you bring a microphone?"

"A good photographer is always prepared."

Joe grabbed what he needed from the suitcase, and they headed back to Virginia's office.

They entered the social services building and approached the woman behind the desk. She was not the same person they had seen the day before. "Good afternoon. I'm Katie, and this is Joe. We are with Channel 23 News. We'd like to speak with Holly Johnson, please."

The woman picked up her phone and dialed an extension. After a few seconds, she said, "A couple of people from the news station would like to speak with you."

"She'll be with you in just a moment," the woman said.

Holly Johnson walked into the lobby and said, "Hello. It's good to see you again. What can I do for you today?"

"Well, we are putting together a piece on Virginia Hall and could use a statement from one of her colleagues. Would you mind speaking with us on camera?"

Holly hesitated momentarily before saying, "Of course not. Where would you like to film it?"

"I think your office would be a good place," Joe said.

"Sure. Follow me," Holly said before leading them to her office.

The first thing Katie noticed when entering the office was a black leather jacket hanging from a coat hanger in the corner near the door. She looked at

Joe, back at the jacket, and then back at Joe. He nodded and said, "I think you should stand behind your desk. I'll shoot it from the corner here."

Holly stood behind her desk, and Katie stood next to her. Joe lifted his camera and positioned himself so the jacket would be in the frame next to Katie. He pressed record and said, "We're recording."

Katie looked at the camera and said, "This is Katie Novak. I'm here with Holly Johnson, A coworker of Virginia Hall. "Tell us, Holly, what happened the day Virginia and her daughter, Ashley, were shot?"

"Well, I was in my office working when I heard a commotion in the hallway. I stopped to listen and heard someone yell, 'Call 911.' I got up and went to the hallway. Several other people were in the hallway, wondering what had happened by then. A group of people stood by the back door until someone finally went outside. Soon, everyone filtered outside, myself included. That's when we learned the terrible news."

"How long did you work with Virginia?" Katie asked.

"Almost six months."

"What did you think of her?"

"She was a wonderful person. She was my mentor. I wouldn't have lasted in this job without her help."

"Thank you so much for speaking with us today, Holly. I know this is a tough time for everyone here. Reporting for Channel 23 News, this is Katie Novak."

Joe turned off the camera, and Katie said, "Thank you for your time, Holly. I think we have all we need here."

"It was my pleasure," Holly said.

***

When they returned to the car, Katie said, "I don't believe it. That was too easy."

"We didn't prove anything yet," Joe said.

"No, but we have her on tape lying."

"We proved she's a liar, not a killer.'

"What about the leather jacket?"

"Lots of people have leather jackets."

"Why are you being negative now? We found our killer," Katie said.

Joe put his hand on Katie's shoulder and said, "I believe it is very likely that Holly Johnson killed Virginia Hall and shot Ashley. I'm just trying to point out what a prosecutor would say."

"You're right. We need to talk to Gabe about this."

"Okay, but let's have lunch first."

They decided to eat lunch at the hotel's restaurant. After they ordered their food, Katie asked, "Do you think we have enough evidence for Gabe to arrest Holly?"

"I doubt it. I do think there is enough evidence to bring her in for questioning. If they do that, Gabe might just get her to confess or at least say something stupid."

"I hope so. I just can't understand what would motivate her to commit murder."

"Hopefully, we'll find out soon."

After lunch, Joe said, "I'd like to go to the room for a little while and practice healing. Then we can talk to Gabe."

"That's a good idea. I would like to feel the baby again.'

"The whole point of practicing is so you can't feel anything."

"No. The point of practicing is so that other people can't feel anything. I'm your wife. I want to feel everything."

"Okay, my dear. We'll do a little of both."

They went upstairs to their room and sat on the sofa. They held hands and closed their eyes. Soon, Katie could feel her unborn baby. It was still tiny, but it emitted a life force that almost overwhelmed her. A tremendous feeling of joy and gratitude swept over her. Just three and a half months ago, she was a lost soul. Her career was at a standstill, and her love life kept ending in failed relationships.

One fateful event changed her life. She hit Joe with her car. She learned of Joe's incredible healing ability and his ability to stay young despite being over a hundred years old. She then helped Joe learn something he was unaware of: that he was the last in a line of healers stretching back hundreds, if not thousands, of years. These healers could heal others simply by touching them. A whirlwind romance followed, ending with marriage and a baby on the way.

Joe gave Katie ten minutes to experience the baby and said, "Okay, I'm going to try to block you out now."

After a few seconds, Katie lost contact with Joe and the baby. Even though she was sitting next to Joe and holding his hand, she had this feeling that she was alone. She knew she was spoiled. No other woman in the world was able to feel what she felt. Ashley had a taste of it, but she was not pregnant.

After another ten minutes, Joe let go and asked, "What did you feel?"

"I think you have the hang of it now. I felt nothing, not even for a second."

"That's great. Maybe when this is over, I can help other people."

"I look forward to seeing that, Joe."

Chapter 6

Before leaving the hotel, Joe removed the memory card from his camera, and Katie downloaded the video interview she had done with Holly Johnson onto her laptop. She then copied it to a thumb drive. She removed it, inserted another thumb drive, and copied the interview video to it along with the videos Gabe gave them. Joe put the memory card back in his camera. Katie put both drives in her purse, and they headed to the police station. When they arrived, an officer escorted them to Gabe's office.

They sat in chairs in front of Gabe's desk, and he asked, "Did you learn something today?"

"We think we know who the murderer is," Katie said.

Gabe looked surprised and said, "Really? Already? Who is it?"

"Holly Johnson," Katie said.

"Virginia's coworker? What makes you suspect her?" Gabe asked.

"Well, first of all, Ashley remembered being shot by someone in a blue ski mask and a black leather jacket. She also remembered her mother showed her a folder that had something to do with the deaths of homeless people."

"And you're just telling me that now?" Gabe said.

"Sorry, but we were a little busy, and it slipped our minds," Katie said. "Were you able to get Victoria's client records?"

"Yes, we did, but I haven't had a chance to look through them."

"Did you check her office? Did you find a folder that she might have shown Ashley?" Katie asked.

"We did check her office and Ashley's car. We didn't find any folder about homeless deaths."

"That's suspicious," Joe said. "The killer probably took it. Check to see if one of Victoria's homeless clients has died recently."

"Okay, I will, but back to Holly Johnson. What evidence do you have that she is involved?"

"It's better if we show you," Joe said. "Bring up the video of Virginia's office. The one pointing at her office door."

Gabe brought up the video while Joe and Katie walked around to his side of the desk. Joe pointed at the screen and said, "This is Holly's door. Watch it closely."

Shortly after Ashley arrived and entered her mother's office, Gabe watched Holly's door crack open and asked, "How is this relevant?"

"Keep watching," Joe said.

A few minutes later, they watched Ashley and Virginia leave. A few seconds after that, they saw Holly's door open all the way.

"So she left her office. How does that make her a killer?"

"Two reasons," Katie said. "First, she lied about where she was when the commotion started, and the second reason should become obvious when you see this video."

Katie handed Gabe the thumb drive. He inserted it into his computer and brought up the video of Katie's interview with Holly. Gabe immediately noticed the leather jacket and said, "I don't believe it."

"Keep watching. You'll see her lie again about where she was," Katie said.

After it was over, Gabe said, "That was good work. You not only caught her in a lie on tape, but you also got the leather jacket in the frame. I wish I had you two on my team."

"We are on your team, Gabe," Katie said."

"Yes, you are, but you know what I mean."

"What will you do now?" Joe asked.

"I need to talk to Ashley again and get her statement about the leather jacket and whatever else she remembers. I think then we can bring Holly in for questioning."

"Can you call us before you do that?" Katie asked. "We'd like to be there."

"It's the least I can do," Gabe said.

***

After leaving Gabe's office, they decided to go to the television station. When they walked into the newsroom, several people greeted them. They told Katie how happy they were that she was back and congratulated them on their wedding. Katie found her desk the way she left it. She checked her email and was overwhelmed by how much was in it. She skimmed through it but found nothing important. "Let's go talk to Billy," she said.

Katie and Joe found Billy tapping away at his computer. She tapped him on his shoulder, and he turned and said, "Oh, Miss Katie. Welcome back. Mr. Martin told me to expect a visit from you."

"Thanks, Billy. It's good to be back, and it's Mrs. now."

"That's right. Congratulations. How can I help you?"

"Two things, Billy. We need information on a woman named Holly Johnson. She's a caseworker at Social Services. We also need to know about the recent deaths of homeless people. Can you find out who died in Milwaukee over the last five months or so?"

"The first one should be easy, but I'm pretty sure deaths are not recorded based on a person's housing status. That might take some time."

"Maybe you can look at which burials were funded by the city. I'm sure these people didn't have insurance or a pre-paid funeral plan. If they were homeless, they probably had no family to help with those expenses."

"That's a great idea. I'll email you when I find something. Do you still have the same email?"

"Yes, I do. Thanks, Billy."

They left Billy and went to Bob Martin's office. Katie knocked on the door, opened it, and asked, "Are you busy?"

"Katie. Joe. Come on in. Have a seat. I'm always busy, but I have time for you."

They sat down, and Bob said, "That was a great interview you did with Ashley. We are getting a lot of positive feedback on our social media channels."

"Thanks, Bob," Katie said.

"So, how's the investigation going?"

"We believe we know who the murderer is," Katie said.

"That was quick. Show me what you have."

Katie took the thumb drive out of her purse and handed it to Bob. He put it in his computer while Katie told him what they learned from Ashley. Joe then explained the videos as he did with Gabe.

"I'm impressed with how you figured this out, but it's not enough to convict her."

"We know, but Gabe will be bringing her in for questioning. We hope he will get her to talk or at least say something that incriminates herself."

"What will you do if she says nothing?"

"We'll just keep plugging along. Billy is looking into a couple of things for us."

"Okay. That's good work, you two. Keep me posted, and let me know if there's anything I can do."

"Okay, thank you," Katie said.

When they left Bob Martin's office, Katie returned to her desk and started rummaging through the drawers. "What are you looking for?" Joe asked.

She found what she was looking for and showed Joe a half dozen business cards. "I was hoping I hadn't thrown them all away."

"That should help our investigation," Joe said.

"Very funny. A business card helps us look more professional. It also makes it easier to share my phone number with someone in case they come across information that might be useful. Don't tell me you never had business cards."

"I'm sorry. I was joking. I didn't expect you to be so passionate about it. I actually have business cards now," Joe said.

"You're kidding? A man with no phone has business cards?"

"Sure, they are at the front desk of the resort."

"Oh, of course. That makes sense. I sometimes forget that you are more like a normal person when you're at the resort."

"What do you mean by a normal person? I think I feel insulted," Joe said.

Katie put her arms around Joe and said, "I love that you're not normal."

"Thanks. I think."

As they left the newsroom, they passed a woman holding her wrist and wincing in pain. "What's wrong, Debbie?" Katie asked.

"Oh, this damn carpal tunnel is kicking my ass today."

"Let me help," Joe said and put his hand on her arm. "There are certain pressure points that might help relieve the pain." He randomly pressed on a spot on her forearm. He had no idea if there really were pressure points, but that didn't matter. After five minutes, he let go. "How does it feel now?"

"She turned her wrist several times and said, "Oh, my God. The pain is almost gone. I don't believe it. Thank you so much."

"I'm glad I could help," Joe said.

As they left the building, Katie said, "What you did was very nice."

"It was a temporary fix. She needs to change her work habits if she wants the pain to stay away."

"Temporary or not, that was a good thing you did."

They got in the car just as Katie's phone rang. She saw it was Gabe calling and answered it. "Hi, Gabe."

"Hi, Katie. I'll be heading with an officer to pick up Holly Johnson for questioning. We'll be there around 4:30. As a courtesy, I'm letting you know, but you can't be part of it."

After she hung up, she repeated to Joe what Gabe said. He looked at the clock on the dashboard and said. "We should have plenty of time to get there."

***

They headed to the social services building and parked in front. After five minutes, Gabe arrived in a police car with a young officer. Joe grabbed his camera from the back seat, and they got out and met Gabe in front of the building. "You need to wait out here," He told them before entering the building.

Gabe and the officer walked past the reception area without saying a word and knocked on Holly's door. Gabe opened the door without waiting for a reply and walked inside with the officer. Holly had a shocked look on her face and asked, "What's going on? What is this all about?"

"Holly Johnson, we need you to come with us to the police station. We have some questions we'd like you to answer."

"Are you arresting me?" she asked.

"Should I be?" Gabe asked.

"Of course not," she said as she stood up. "I'll cooperate any way that I can."

She put her leather jacket on, and the officer grabbed her arm. She stomped on his foot, causing him to let go of her and wince in pain as Holly raced out the door. She ran outside onto the street, where a pickup truck ran into her. Joe filmed the whole thing and handed the camera to Katie before running to see if Holly was okay. She lay on the ground, apparently unconscious, while a crowd gathered. The young officer got on his radio and called for an ambulance while

Joe knelt, touched her arm, and pretended to examine her. After thirty seconds, he let go and returned to Katie.

"Why did you stop?" she asked. "What's wrong?"

"Nothing's wrong," Joe said. "She's not hurt badly. She's faking it."

"She's faking it? Why would she do that?"

"I don't know. That truck slowed her down. She probably figured they would catch her and thinks a hospital would be easier to escape from than a jail."

"That makes sense. What will you tell Gabe?"

"Nothing. I can't tell him that she's faking an injury. How would I explain knowing that?"

Katie shook her head. "I don't know. We should give him the heads up somehow."

Joe walked over to where Gabe was standing. Katie followed him. "Gabe," he said. "I don't trust her. I assume you will post someone at her door at the hospital."

"Of course," Gabe said.

"You should also handcuff her to the bed."

"Don't worry. She won't get past us again."

A few minutes later, an ambulance and several more police officers arrived. They put Holly into the ambulance and drove her away. Katie and Joe learned from Gabe that the ambulance was taking her to the same hospital where Ashley was. When they were alone, Katie said, "I have a bad feeling about this."

Joe nodded and said, "Yeah, me too."

***

Once back at the hotel, Katie took out her laptop and checked her emails. She got one from Billy and opened it. "Billy sent us something," she said.

Joe stood behind Katie and looked over her shoulder. She opened the first attachment. It was about Holly Johnson. "It says Holly earned her bachelor's degree in social work, but didn't work in the field after college. Instead, she went to nursing school and became a nurse. She was a nurse at Jackson McCormick Hospital for seven years. Maybe that's why she faked being

49

unconscious. Maybe she knew she would be taken there. Maybe she has friends there that could help her escape."

"That makes a lot of sense," Joe said. "What else does it say about her?"

"Her father died almost a year ago, and she quit her job a couple of months after that."

"Does it say how her father died?"

"No. There are no details here about that."

"Can you ask Billy to look into it for us?"

"Certainly," Katie said and replied to the email with the request.

Katie opened the other attachment and started to read it to herself. After a while, Joe said, "What does it say?"

"It says there have been 16 deaths of people with no listed address since five months ago. It looks like Billy found a better way to search than I suggested."

"He does that for a living," Joe said.

"It's still impressive. It also says the average is usually less than two a month. So, since five months ago, there have been six or seven more deaths of homeless people than average."

"Does that report say when Holly started working for Social Services?"

Katie looked at the screen and said, "Next week will be six months."

"So, Holly Johnson takes a job at Social Services, and suddenly, homeless people start dying. Why would that be?"

"I don't know. Maybe she hates homeless people for some reason."

"Does it say anything else about her in that report? I mean, was she attacked or something like that?"

"No. There are no police reports. I don't think Billy would have missed that."

"It just doesn't add up," Joe said. "She went to school for social work, and then she went to nursing school. Both professions indicate a desire to help people, not kill them."

"Sometimes people snap," Katie said.

"Sometimes they do, but in this case, I feel like we're missing a piece of the puzzle."

"We should talk to the medical examiner tomorrow. If we can find out why those people died, we might have a better understanding of what's going on around here."

"Did Billy send you a list of names?" Joe asked.

"Yes, he did. The most recent was a man named Timothy Edelson. He died four days before Ashley and Virginia were shot. It's possible his death is what prompted Virginia to call Ashley and ask for her help. We should start with him."

"I agree. Maybe you can ask Gabe if this Edelson guy was a client of hers."

"I'll text him," Katie said before taking out her phone and typing a message to Gabe.

She put her phone away and said, "I'm starving. We should get something to eat."

"I would like to spend some quality time with my beautiful wife," Joe said. "I bet we can order food from the hotel restaurant and have it delivered to the room."

Katie put her arms around Joe and kissed him. "I love the way you think."

When they finished eating, they took a bath together. As they lay in the tub, Katie asked, "Do you think I'll be an okay mom?"

"No. I think you'll be a great mom. Do you have doubts?"

"I don't know. This is new to me. You've been through it before, but I'm not sure what to do. What if I screw up? What if our child becomes a criminal because I was too strict or too lenient?"

"Are you thinking about Holly Johnson's mother?"

"Yes. Whatever she did wrong, I don't want to do that."

"Relax. I'm certain you will be a great mother. The thing is, no matter what you do, there will always be influences that are beyond your control. The best you can do is be an example of what a good person should be. For you, that will be easy."

Katie leaned back against Joe's chest, looked up, and said, "I'm so glad I married you."

Chapter 7

Katie and Joe woke up the following morning when Katie's phone rang. She picked it up and looked at the screen. It was Gabe. "Good morning, Gabe."

"Good morning, Katie. You sound tired. Did I wake you up?"

"Yes, but it's okay. We were up late last night."

"You were? What did you do?"

"Gabe, I'm certain I mentioned that we're newlyweds."

"Oh, yes, of course. Stupid question. I'm sorry for waking you."

"It's fine. What's going on?"

"Holly Johnson is dead."

"What?" Katie said loud enough to get Joe's attention.

"What happened?" Joe asked.

"Holly Johnson is dead."

"What?"

Katie hit the speaker button on her phone and said, "I have you on speaker, Gabe. What happened?"

"Apparently, her injuries were worse than we thought."

"No. Absolutely not," Joe said. "Her injuries were not life-threatening."

"How do you know, Joe? Are you a doctor now?"

"No. Not exactly. You'll have to trust me on this, Gabe. Either the doctor who treated her screwed up big time, or she was murdered."

"Murdered? That's a stretch. Who would want to murder her?"

"I don't know," Joe said, "but you need to find out who had access to her while she was in the hospital."

"Okay. I think your assumption is out there in left field, but it won't hurt to do a little digging. On another note, how did you know Timothy Edelson was a client of Victoria's, Katie?"

"I didn't know. That's why I asked."

"I mean, where did you learn that name?"

"He was on a list of recently deceased homeless people that we got from a researcher at the station."

"I have that same list. Two on the list were clients of Virginia's, and two more were clients of Holly's. I don't have information on other caseworkers in that office."

"That would explain why Virginia wanted Ashley's help to start an investigation. She probably felt the police would consider it a coincidence," Katie said.

"She may have been right in that assumption," Gabe said. "It's a shame, but many homeless people die younger than average. Without further evidence, this probably would have been dismissed as a coincidence."

"We're going this morning to talk to the medical examiner. Maybe learning the cause of death will be helpful," Katie said.

"Good idea. I'll come with you. It's a little after eight now. How about I pick you up at your hotel at ten?"

"Okay, Gabe. That sounds good. We'll be ready."

Katie and Joe were ready in an hour, giving them enough time to eat breakfast at the hotel restaurant. They then met Gabe in the parking lot and headed to the coroner's office.

When they arrived, Gabe showed his badge and asked to speak to the medical examiner. A thin, older man with thick, white hair met them. He held out his hand and said, "Hi, I'm Dr. Adams."

They all shook hands, and Gabe said, "I'm Captain Garcia, and this is Joe and Katie Novak. They are reporters. We're working on a case together."

He invited them into his office and sat behind his desk. Only two chairs were in front of his desk, so they all chose to stand. "What can I do for you?" he asked.

We'd like some information on a few recent deaths," Katie said. "Let's start with a woman named Olivia Park."

The doctor tapped away at his computer and said, "It says here that she died from a traumatic brain injury." He continued reading and said, "It says she was hit by a car while crossing the street."

"Is there anything in there about who hit her?" Katie asked.

"That type of information wouldn't be on the autopsy report," Dr. Adams said.

"Did you not do the autopsy?" Joe asked.

"No, I didn't, so I'm afraid I can only tell you what it says, but I assume you can find that information in the police report."

Katie and Joe looked at Gabe, who said, "This is the first I've heard of it. I'll check when I get back to the station."

"Can we speak to the medical examiner who did the autopsy?" Joe asked.

"That would be Dr. Diane Rand. She works the night shift. She comes in at six."

"What about Timothy Edelson. Can you check that name, Doc?" Katie asked.

The doctor tapped a few keys and said, "Timothy Edelson died from an overdose of fentanyl."

"Who did that autopsy?" Joe asked.

Dr. Adams looked at the screen and said, That was also Dr. Rand."

Joe and Katie looked at each other, and then Katie asked Gabe, "Who were the two victims who were clients of Holly Johnson?"

Gabe looked at a printout and said, "Kevin Brown and Robert Grossman. Can you look up those two names, Doc?"

The doctor tapped on his keyboard and said, "It looks like Kevin Brown is another fentanyl overdose." He tapped a few more keys. "Robert Grossman died from a heart attack."

"You didn't do any of these autopsies?" Gabe asked.

"No. They were all performed by Dr. Rand."

"Do you find it unusual, Doctor, that she performed all the autopsies we came here to discuss?" Katie asked.

"Yes. It's quite a coincidence. I know that the night shift tends to be more efficient because they have fewer distractions, which might account for it."

What about Holly Johnson?" Gabe asked. "When will you do the autopsy on her?"

"The doctor checked his computer and said, "She just arrived here this morning. She's scheduled to be examined by Dr. Rand tonight."

"No, not her," Joe said. "We need you to do it."

"I'm sorry, but I have priorities. Dr. Rand is a well-qualified physician. I trust her to do a good job despite the recent coincidences. If you don't trust her, I suggest you sit in on the autopsy. It is her first scheduled for tonight."

"Okay, Doctor. We appreciate your time," Katie said.

Gabe drove Katie and Joe back to their hotel and said, "I'll check for any police reports on our victims. We can meet at the coroner's office at six and talk to Dr. Rand."

"Sounds good," Katie said. "I think we'll go check on Ashley."

"Okay. Give her my best," Gabe said.

***

Katie and Joe didn't go back to their room. Instead, they walked to Katie's car. She checked her phone first and saw an email from Billy. "Billy sent us something about Holly Johnson's father. It says he died at the hospital where she worked while he was waiting for a heart transplant. I'm not sure why she would quit her job because of that. Do you think she blamed the hospital for some reason?"

"That's a possibility, but I think getting access to a donor's heart is out of the hospital's control. I'm not sure, but I thought they had some kind of committee that prioritized who would get the next heart. "

"I think you're right. I believe it's based on who has the best chance to survive and live a long life."

"I wouldn't want that burden," Joe said. "Imagine having to choose who lives and who dies."

"I agree. What a terrible responsibility that would be," Katie said.

Katie started the engine, and they headed to Ashley's house. On the way, Katie said, "I hope you don't mind seeing Ashley right now. You did say you wanted to get her to a hundred percent, and this might be a good time."

"If she's alone, this would be a great time to finish what we started," Joe said.

Ashley's house was a few miles southwest of the downtown area. It was a two-story structure with an attic. The house was sandwiched between similar-looking houses. It was painted white with dark red trim. Joe thought it looked well cared for. Katie rang the doorbell, and after fifteen seconds, Ashley opened the door. She looked excited to see them and said, "Katie! Joe! I didn't expect you. Come on in."

She stepped aside to let Katie and Joe in. The home was clean but not entirely tidy. It was clear that children lived there. Several coloring books and crayons lay on an end table, and a video game system was on the coffee table with cords running to the television. Joe liked the old hardwood floors and said so. "These are nice floors."

"Thanks," Ashley said." "The house is eighty years old, and I'm pretty sure these are the original floors. I think they held up quite well."

"They sure did," Joe said.

"I assume you didn't come here to look at my floors."

"Are you alone?" Katie asked.

"Yes. The kids are at school, and John is at work. I convinced him that I would be fine."

"I thought we could remove those remaining bullet fragments today," Joe said.

"I would love to get those out of me. Will it hurt?"

"You will feel a little pain, but I'll feel it too. We'll do it together. Do you have a comfortable place that won't get ruined by a little blood?"

"How about the leather sofa? I can put a towel down. That should be good enough."

"That will work," Joe said.

Ashley went into another room and came out with a large beach towel that she draped over the sofa. She sat on the towel, and Joe sat next to her. "I'll need to raise your shirt up in the back," Joe said.

"No. I like this shirt. I don't want to get blood on it. I'll just take it off."

Joe looked at Katie, who shrugged.

Asley noticed the tension and said, "For Pete's sake. You felt me from the inside out, and now you have an issue seeing me in my bra?"

Joe looked at Katie again, who nodded. "Okay, Ashley, go ahead."

Ashley removed her shirt and handed it to Katie, who draped it over a chair. Joe held her hand and said, "Okay, stay like this. Don't lean back."

He didn't try to block Ashley out this time. He thought it would be good for her to feel what was happening. He found the bullet fragments and instructed her body to push them out. Slowly, they worked their way to her back and pushed through her skin. There was some blood, but Joe shifted his focus to clotting the blood where the pieces broke the skin."

He stopped momentarily and asked Katie to get a warm, wet cloth. When she returned, she gently wiped Ashley's back. When she finished, Ashley stood while Katie picked up the towel with the bullet fragments. "Do you want to save these for a memento?" Katie asked.

"Hell, no. Throw that damn thing in the trash. I don't need any reminders."

Ashley put her shirt back on and sat back on the sofa. Joe continued with the healing. He wanted to erase the scars as much as possible. After about an hour, Joe let go and said, "I think I've done all I can do for you. You should be fine now."

Ashley hugged Joe and said, "Thank you so much for everything you've done." She got up and hugged Katie, who was sitting on the other side of Joe. "I love you guys. You must be hungry. Can I make you some lunch?"

"If you don't mind, that would be great," Katie said.

"Mind? Don't be silly. It's my pleasure."

Ashley got up and went to the kitchen. She opened the refrigerator and asked, " How do you feel about chicken and vegetable soup? John made a big pot for me yesterday. I think he thought I was recovering from a cold instead of a gunshot wound."

"His intentions were good," Katie said.

"Yes. John is an intelligent man, but sometimes he lacks common sense. I can't complain, though, because his intentions are always good, and I love him to death. "

She took the pot from the refrigerator and heated it on the stove. They sat at the dining room table and talked. Soon, the smell of the soup reached Katie's nose. "Oh, my God! I don't believe it. It smells just like Joe's cabin the day I hit him with my car."

"That's right," Joe said. "Smells can bring back memories even better than sights or sounds."

"You told me it was an old family recipe, and I thought you were too young to pick up old family recipes."

They both laughed, and Ashley asked, "Why is that funny? He is pretty young."

Katie looked at Joe and asked, "Should we tell her?"

Joe shrugged and said, "You may as well. She knows everything else." Ashley looked confused and said, "What? What do you want to tell me?"

"Well, Joe is older than you think. A lot older."

"Really? You're not going to tell me he's forty, are you?"

Katie looked at Joe, smiled, and said, "No. He's definitely not forty. Joe was born in 1916."

Ashley laughed and said, "That's funny."

I'm serious," Katie said. "You know Joe has the ability to heal. He is able to heal himself from aging."

Ashley looked at Joe and asked, "Is that really true?"

"It's true," Joe said.

"That's amazing. How did you get those abilities anyway? Are they hereditary? Are your parents like you?"

These abilities are hereditary, but they are also rare. The last person to have them was my great-grandfather."

"So your parents were normal?"

"I don't know if anybody is truly normal, but my parents did not have what I have. My mother died at childbirth, and my father died in the war before I was born."

"The war? You mean World War One?"

"Yes. We called it The Great War until it happened again."

"Wait a minute. I know a little about history, and we didn't get into the war until the following year."

"If by 'we' you mean America, that is correct, but my parents were Croatian. After my father died, my mother managed to escape to America. I was born the day the ship landed in New York."

"Wow. That explains a lot. I mean, no wonder you have such great manners. You were raised at a time when people cared about those things."

"People have changed over the last hundred years, but there have always been good and bad people, and there always will be," Joe said.

"I think the soup is ready," Ashley said before getting up and scooping it into three bowls. She added spoons and brought them to the table.

Joe tasted the soup and said, "This is very good."

"It's delicious. It tastes like Joe's soup," Katie said.

"Maybe John's family got the recipe from Joe's family," Ashley said.

"Actually, my recipe came from my wife's family." Joe looked at Katie and added, "I mean, my first wife's family."

"Joe was married before me," Katie said. "He has a big family with kids and grandkids, all the way to great great grandkids."

Ashley looked at Joe and said, "That is incredible. Looking at you, it just doesn't seem possible."

"I have been lucky," Joe said, "but if I had grown old and died with my first wife, I would have still felt like I lived a great life." He put his hand on Katie's and said, "Now I feel like I am at the beginning of a second great life."

"Well, I'm happy for you both. I'll be even happier seeing little baby Katie or baby Joe."

"With everything that has happened, we haven't even thought of a name yet," Katie said.

"If I had another child, I would name him or her after one of you."

"I think it would be great to have a little Katie Junior," Joe said.

Katie slapped him on the arm and said, "Very funny."

When they finished eating, Katie and Joe helped clean up, and Katie said, "Thanks for lunch, Ashley. It was way better than going out."

"Thanks again for everything," Ashley said. "By the way, Mom's funeral is Saturday. I hope you'll be there.

Katie hugged Ashley and said, "Of course, we will."

Ashley wrote down the information and gave it to Katie. They all hugged again before Joe and Katie left.

***

"I'm happy that Ashley is back to normal now," Joe said as they got into the car.

"I am, too. I feel like I can be happy again about the baby. Let's go back to the hotel for a while. I think it's time we tell my parents the news, and I don't want to do it from the car."

When they returned to their room, they sat beside each other, and Katie dialed her parents' number. She tapped the speaker button and held the phone in front of her.

Katie's mother answered and said, "Hi, Dear. How's married life?"

"It's great, Mom. I have Joe here with me."

"Oh, hi, Joe. It was so nice visiting with you. I can't believe you chose to come here for your honeymoon."

"It was nice visiting with you, too, Mary," Joe said. "I wanted to get to know my wife better. I thought getting to know her family and seeing where she grew up would be a great way to do that."

"It also gave us a chance to get to know you, too, Joe. I think Katie was lucky to find you."

"I think we were both lucky," Joe said.

"So, are you settling into your new job, okay, Dear?"

"I haven't had a chance to do much yet," Katie said. "We're in Milwaukee now. My friend Ashley was shot, and we came to be with her."

"Oh, my! Is she okay?"

"She's okay now, but her mother was killed."

"Oh, that's terrible. Please give her my condolences."

"I will, Mom. I actually have some other news that I need Dad to hear, too. Is he there?"

"He's in the other room. Karl, come here. Katie and Joe are on the phone. He can hear you now. Go ahead."

"Well, we're just calling to let you know we're going to have a baby."

Mary screamed, "Oh, I'm so happy. You both will make wonderful parents."

"Congratulations, you two," Karl said. "I can't wait to spoil her with sugar and then send her home like your grandma did."

"You're so funny, Dad. I wasn't that spoiled."

"If you say so, Kiddo."

"Besides, it might be a boy."

"Even better. We could go fishing together."

"How's the baby doing?" Mary asked. "What did the doctor say?"

"I haven't been to a doctor."

"Oh, so you took one of those home pregnancy tests?"

Katie looked at Joe, who smiled. "Yes. I guess you could call it that."

"Well, you should visit a doctor soon. You don't want to have any complications."

Katie put her hand on Joe's and said, "There is a man who lives very close to me who can help with that."

"That's good to hear, Dear. I'm so glad you called us with the good news. Again, tell your friend I am so sorry to hear about her mom."

They all said goodbye, and Katie hung up the phone. She leaned against Joe, who put his arm around her. "You know, I was thinking about how I would feel if someone killed my mom, and I realized that I didn't give Ashley nearly enough sympathy."

"Everything is always less painful when it happens to other people," Joe said.

"How did you get so wise? Never mind, don't answer that."

They sat quietly together for a while, and then Joe said, "We will probably be at the coroner's office for a while. We should eat something first."

"You're right," Katie said. "Let's order Chinese food."

Katie asked Joe what he wanted and called to place an order for delivery. When the food arrived, they sat on the balcony and ate it. They had a nice view of the city, and Joe asked, "Do you miss living here?"

"Not at all. I thought I would, but I have learned that who I am with is way more important than where I am."

"How did you get so wise?" Joe asked. "Never mind, don't answer that."

Katie slapped Joe on the arm and said, "I hope you're not implying I'm old."

"You implied it about me."

"Because you are old."

"You are over thirty. Listening to you on your birthday made me think your life was almost over."

"I said no such thing. I think you have memory problems in your old age."

"Okay, my mistake. It must have been another thirty-year-old that I'm sleeping with."

Katie slapped Joe on the arm again and said, "Don't even joke about something like that."

"Okay. I'm sorry."

Katie kissed him and said, "I hope you will always apologize when you know you're wrong."

***

At six, they met Gabe in front of the coroner's office and went inside. Gabe showed his badge and asked to speak with Dr. Rand. A couple of minutes later, Dr. Rand came out to greet them. She was an attractive woman in her

61

mid-thirties with red hair and blue eyes. "I'm Dr. Rand," she said, holding out her hand.

"They shook hands, and Gabe said, "I'm Captain Garcia with the Milwaukee Police Department. This is Katie and Joe Novak with Channel 23 News. We are working together on a case."

"Of course," Dr. Rand said. "Follow me. We can talk in my office."

She led them to her office and sat at her desk. "What can I help you with?" she asked.

"We are investigating the rise in homeless deaths lately. We came here earlier today to ask about four people in particular and learned you performed the autopsy on all four." Gabe handed her a piece of paper with the names on it.

She read the names on the paper and said, "Yes. I recognize these names. What do you need to know about them?"

"We think it's quite a coincidence that you performed all four of those autopsies," Joe said. "Why is that?"

"Well, Mr. Novak. You have to understand the dynamics of this office. The day shift is under a lot of pressure from people like you: police officers, reporters, attorneys, etc. They want answers right away, so the less important cases, like the people on your list, get pushed down to the night shift, and since I am the only doctor on the night shift, I get them all. Plus, I get through more cases because I am usually not interrupted, no offense."

"We'd like to interrupt you more by observing the Autopsy of Holly Johnson," Joe said.

"It sounds like you don't trust me," Dr. Rand said.

"We do have doubts," Joe said.

"Do any of you have medical knowledge?" The doctor asked. "If I were to fake a result, would you even know it? You are welcome to watch if you want, but it will take a while and could get quite unpleasant if you're not used to it. We record every autopsy. I would happily give you a copy of Holly Johnson's autopsy and the other four you mentioned. You can show them to an expert if you want."

They all looked at each other, and Katie said, "I really wasn't looking forward to this. I say we skip it."

"Okay," Gabe said. "He handed Dr. Rand a business card and said, "Call me as soon as you know something."

"Okay, but don't expect anything for at least two hours, maybe three."

They all left the office, and Katie asked, "What should we do for the next two or three hours? Joe and I ate dinner already."

"I did too," Gabe said, "but there's always dessert. I know a place not far from here that makes good pies."

"Now you're talking my language, Gabe," Katie said.

They followed Gabe to a small diner called Suzie's Kitchen. It was decorated in a retro style to resemble a 1950s diner. They sat in a booth near a window. Katie and Gabe ordered a slice of apple pie and a coffee, while Joe ordered the pecan pie and a glass of orange juice.

After they got their drinks, Katie said, "I'm going to turn you into a coffee drinker if it takes a hundred years."

"Maybe in a hundred years, someone will discover a coffee bean that tastes like orange juice," Joe said.

"Yeah. I'm sure that will happen."

"My wife doesn't like coffee either, but I love her anyway," Gabe said.

Katie put her arm around Joe and said, "I love Joe too, despite his obvious faults."

The server arrived with their pies and set them on the table. When she left, Katie took a bite of her pie and said, "You're right, Gabe, this is delicious."

"I come here with my wife sometimes," Gabe said. "Her store is not too far from here."

"That's right. Your wife designs jewelry," Katie said. "We talked to her for a while at our wedding. She showed pictures of some of her creations. They really are beautiful."

"She's quite talented," Gabe said.

They sat and talked for a couple of hours until Gabe's phone rang. He answered, saying, "Hello. This is Captain Garcia."

"Hello, Captain Garcia. This is Dr. Rand. I have the cause of death. We can review it if you'd like to return now."

"We'll be there in ten minutes," he said.

They got the check, and Joe put money on the table. When they returned to the coroner's office, Dr. Rand met them and invited them into her office. "So, how did Holly Johnson die?" Gabe asked.

"The cause of death is asphyxiation," Dr. Rand said. "None of her injuries would have caused that. Someone suffocated her."

"You mean she was murdered?" Gabe asked.

"That's right. I found white cotton fibers in her mouth. My guess is that someone held a pillow over her face."

"I don't believe it," Gabe said. "It looks like you were right, Joe."

"Do you know what time she died?" Joe asked.

"I would estimate around seven yesterday evening, with a two-hour margin for error."

"I assume you had someone posted at her door," Joe said. "You just need to find out who was in her room between five and nine, especially the last person to enter her room."

"It's getting late," Gabe said. "I need to get home to my wife. I'll look into it in the morning and call you when I learn something."

"Okay, Gabe," Katie said. "Say hi to your wife for us and tell her we're sorry for keeping you out too long."

***

Katie and Joe drove back to the hotel. When Katie parked the car, she said. "I don't want to go to the room yet. Let's take a walk."

"Okay," Joe said as he got out of the car. "I can use the fresh air."

The night air was chilly. A cold breeze came from the lake, so they zipped up their jackets. They held hands as they walked. After walking a couple of blocks, Joe asked, "Is something bothering you, Katie?"

"No. There's nothing wrong. I've just been thinking about our future."

"Our future? You mean about the baby?"

"Partly, but also about us. I feel like I'm ready to settle down and have a normal life."

"I totally agree," Joe said, "but I thought we were already doing that. We bought a house, got married, and now we have a child on the way. Isn't that what normal people do?"

They reached the shore of Lake Michigan. A pedestrian trail ran along the lake, and next to the trail was a park bench. "Let's sit down," Katie said.

They sat on the bench, and Joe put his arm around Katie to help keep her warm. She snuggled close and asked, "Do you remember when we were here last?"

"Sure. It was our first and last case together, not counting this one. It happened just a little bit that way," Joe said, pointing to the right.

"That way," Katie said, pointing to the left. "That poor Williams couple were murdered for trying to do the right thing. We couldn't bring them back, but we brought their killer to justice. We did that. It was the first meaningful thing I did in my life up until then."

"We did a good thing, Katie. What's the problem?"

"There's no problem. It's just that if we want to be normal, we can't keep involving ourselves in murder investigations."

"This is only our second case. It's not like it's a habit. We can stop if you want and go home. Ashley is okay now. We did what we came here to do."

"That's the problem, Joe. I don't want to stop."

Joe looked out at the lake, realizing what Katie was trying to say. "Oh, I see now. You want to settle down and be normal, but you are worried that a normal life will be boring."

"I have mixed feelings right now, but what you say is close to the truth."

Joe hugged her tighter and said, "Don't worry. I'm certain no rule exists that says normal has to be boring. I won't lie. It can be challenging to do everything you want while raising children, but I'm sure you'll find time to do those things that bring you happiness. Hopefully, we can find a good substitute for hunting down murderers."

"Yeah. Maybe we can hunt down those elusive lost socks that all those normal people have a problem with."

"That's the spirit," Joe said. "Now, let's head back and get into that warm bed. I have some investigating I want to do."

"Oh, you dirty old man. Okay, let's hurry."

Chapter 8

Katie and Joe woke up with the sun the next morning. They got ready and had breakfast in the hotel restaurant again. They hadn't heard anything from Gabe that morning, so when they finished eating, Katie called him.

"Good morning, Katie," he said.

"Good morning, Gabe. I'm here with Joe. I have you on speaker. Did you learn anything about who was in Holly's room when she died?"

"I spoke with my guy this morning. He said her mother was in the room last. She noticed her daughter was cold and alerted the staff."

"Oh, wow! That must have been heartbreaking for her."

"No doubt," Gabe said. "Before the mother went in, a cleaning lady went in to clean the room. Before that, the hospital administrator went in, and a nurse was there before that. A doctor was also in her room, but my guy was unsure about who was before whom. He wasn't there to keep track of people."

"That's understandable, but wouldn't the alarm on her monitor go off when her heart stopped beating?" Joe asked.

"She wasn't hooked up to any machine," Gabe said. "Anybody who went in there would just assume she was unconscious."

"Why wasn't she hooked up to a monitor?" Katie asked.

"I called the hospital administrator and asked that very question. He said the doctor who examined her decided she was stable and the monitor was unnecessary."

"Sounds like someone screwed up, and he doesn't want the hospital to get sued," Joe said.

"Can you get us the names of all the people you mentioned? We'd like to talk to them," Katie said.

"Sure, but I plan on doing that," Gabe said.

"Okay, let us know what you learn. In the meantime, we'd still like those names so we can do our own research," Katie said.

"Okay, Gabe said. I will email them to you in a few minutes."

When Katie hung up, she said, "Let's go back to our room."

"What do you want to do there?"

"I want to have sex. What do you think?"

"Really?"

Katie ran her fingers through Joe's thick, dark hair and said, "You are so cute. I think I spoil you too much. I want to go upstairs so we can strategize."

"You want to strategize while we're having sex?" Joe asked and laughed.

"I definitely spoil you too much," Katie said.

When they got to their room, Katie sat next to Joe on the bed, opened her laptop, and checked her email. The email from Gabe with the names of the people who were in Holly's room was there. She read it, then forwarded it to Billy and asked if he could get information about the people on the list. She set the laptop next to her and said, "So we need to figure out why someone would want to kill Holly."

"I think the obvious answer is she was part of a conspiracy. When she got caught, the other person or persons decided to prevent her from talking to the police."

"Exactly, but what could this conspiracy be about? Why would anyone want to kill homeless people?

"I don't know. My first thought was a group of disgruntled business owners, but Holly wasn't a business owner."

"No, she wasn't. Perhaps she was a hired killer, and the caseworker job was a cover," Katie said.

"That's a bit far-fetched," Joe said.

"I know. I was just throwing stuff out there, hoping something would stick."

I think we need to take that medical examiner up on her offer and look at those autopsy videos," Joe said.

"Do you still think she's part of this?" Katie asked. "She did say someone murdered Holly. She would have covered up that fact if she were part of this."

"There's a good chance she is telling the truth, but she could also be throwing another conspirator under the bus."

"Do you think you know enough to tell if she is faking something?"

"No. Definitely not. I have, however, picked up people's patterns over the years. I can sometimes tell if someone is acting suspiciously. I'm not an expert, but I think I read people pretty well, and the doctor doesn't seem to be hiding anything."

"Well, I guess we'll see. Let's head back to the coroner's office and see if we can get those videos."

***

When they arrived, they spoke to the same medical examiner they had spoken to the previous morning. Katie said, "Dr. Rand told us all the autopsies performed here are recorded. She also said we could get a copy of those recordings. How do we do that?"

The doctor said, "We have them on an internal server that you can access online. They are unavailable to the general public, but I can send you a link to each one. Which names do you need?"

Katie handed him a paper with the names on it. He looked at it and asked, "Do you have a business card?"

Katie reached into her purse and handed him one of her business cards. He opened an email, attached the links, and sent them to Katie. "Okay. You should be getting it in your inbox any moment now."

"Thank you so much, Doctor," Katie said.

As they were walking out, Katie said, "See. I told you those business cards would come in handy."

"You were right, Katie. Without a business card, there would be no way you could have given your email address to that doctor."

Katie gave Joe a dirty look and said, "Thanks for your support. I'll remember that tonight."

Joe laughed and said, "I'm sorry. Will you forgive me?"

Katie looked at him momentarily and said, "I'll think about it."

They reached Katie's car and got in. She started the engine and said, "So far, so good."

"So far, so good? What do you mean by that?"

"I mean, most men can't admit when they're wrong. So far, you're doing good."

Joe was about to say that he didn't apologize because he was wrong, but decided to keep his mouth shut.

They drove back to the hotel. When they returned to their room, Katie got her laptop and sat on the sofa. Joe sat beside her as she opened her email and clicked on the first link the medical examiner sent her. It was for a man named Robert Grossman. It showed a male body from above. Dr. Rand was speaking. She described everything that she did.

"Can you speed it up?" Joe asked.

Katie found a button that said "Playback Speed" when she hovered over it. She clicked on it and was presented with several options. "How fast do you want it?" she asked.

Joe looked at the options and said, "Let's try the eight times speed."

Katie sped up the video, and they watched it for about fifteen minutes. When it ended, Katie asked, "Did you notice anything unusual?"

"No. Nothing. Did you notice anything?"

"Are you kidding? She'd have to be dissecting a chimpanzee before I would notice anything unusual."

"Let's watch the next one," Joe said.

Katie clicked on the next link, Olivia Park's autopsy. Joe noticed it right away. "Hit pause," he said.

Katie hit the pause button, and Joe asked, "Do you see it?"

"I sure do. Someone already opened this woman up, and it looks recent."

"Let's see the next one," Joe said.

The next one was Timothy Edelson. His body also showed evidence of being cut open before the autopsy. "What the hell?" Katie said.

"Go to the next one," Joe said.

Katie started the video for Kevin Brown's autopsy. He was also cut open and stitched back together. "I don't know what's going on," Katie said, "but we need to talk to that Dr. Rand again tonight."

"I agree," Joe said.

"Right now, though, I'm hungry. Let's go out for lunch," Katie said.

"Okay. Where would you like to eat?"

"I don't care, but I'm tired of the hotel restaurant. Let's try something different."

"We passed an Irish restaurant a couple of miles from here?"

"Irish? I hope you don't mean McDonald's."

"No. Not McDonald's. I think it was called 'Mahony's' or something like that."

"I think I know where that is," Katie said, "but the Irish are not exactly known for their fine cuisine."

"Maybe not, but they should be."

"Seriously?"

"If you are afraid to try new things, we can go somewhere else."

Katie looked at him momentarily and said, "I accept your challenge."

***

Katie drove to the restaurant that was actually called Molony's. They went inside, and a young woman seated them at a table near the center of the restaurant. She put menus on the table and said, "Your server will be with you shortly."

They opened their menus, and after a minute, Joe asked, "Do you see anything you think you would like?"

"I'm not sure what half of this stuff is. Just order something for me that's good."

A young man arrived at their table and said, "Hi, I'm Sean. I'll be taking care of you today."

"Hi, Sean. We know what we want," Joe said, hoping to speed things up a little.

"Okay, sure. What can I get for you?"

"We would like an order of Boxey and two orders of Guinness beef stew."

"Those are good choices. Can I get you something to drink?"

"Two waters, please."

When the server left, Katie asked, "How do you know about Irish food? I mean, where did you first discover it?"

"I don't know when I first tried Irish food, but I learned how good it could be from my oldest son's wife. Her parents were immigrants from Ireland."

"I wish I could have met your sons."

"I'm sure they would have liked you very much. I never told you this, Katie, but you are a lot like their mother was at your age. I think that is partly why I was attracted to you."

"In what ways am I like her?" Katie asked.

"Well, you look similar to her and have that same kind of spunk."

"Spunk?"

"Yes. I don't know how to say it exactly, but you have that take-charge attitude. You're not shy. You're good at comforting people when they need comforting, and you're good at kicking their ass when they need an ass kicking. Verbally speaking, I mean."

"I'm not sure about the ass-kicking part, but I know what you mean. I have noticed I sometimes talk more than you do."

The server showed up and put their appetizer on the table. He said, "Your dinner will be up shortly. Is there anything else I can get for you?"

"No, thank you," Katie said.

After he walked away, Katie said, "Oh, these look like potato pancakes."

"That's basically what they are," Joe said as he placed one on Katie's plate and another on his plate.

Katie took a bite and said, "These are very tasty."

Katie's phone rang. She picked it up and saw it was Gabe. She put it on speaker but turned the volume down halfway. "Hi, Gabe."

"Hi, Katie. Is Joe with you?"

"He's right here. What's going on?"

"I found a police report on Olivia Park. It was a hit-and-run. One witness reported that a blue sedan hit her, but didn't know the make or model. I checked, and Holly drove a blue 2012 Ford Taurus. We inspected her car and found damage to the passenger-side headlight. The damage might have occurred from hitting someone, but there is no way to know for sure."

"So Holly was most likely involved in murdering homeless people," Katie said.

"It seems so," Gabe said. "Although we expected that. Now we just have to find her accomplice."

"Assuming there is only one," Katie said.

"That's right. We don't know how big this thing is," Gabe said.

"Okay, Gabe," Joe said. "Let us know if you learn anything new. We're going to speak with that medical examiner again tonight."

"You are? What about?"

"It could be nothing," Joe said. "We looked at the autopsy recordings and saw something we don't understand."

"I'd go with you, but I've been neglecting my wife too much lately. I promised to take her to a nice restaurant tonight."

"Perhaps she would like German food," Katie said.

"Oh, that's very funny, Katie. I think it would be better for everyone if I found a place with all male waiters."

"Good luck with that," Katie said.

"Thanks a lot."

The server arrived with their food when Katie hung up. When he left, Katie took a bite of her stew and said, "Wow! This is delicious. I will remember this the next time I doubt you."

"That's good because I know a great Australian restaurant that serves the best kangaroo."

"What? Kangaroo? No way. Don't even think about taking me there."

Joe smiled but said nothing.

Chapter 9

After lunch, they got in the car, and Katie asked, "What should we do now?"

"I would like to practice my new healing method. Is there a children's hospital nearby?"

"There's one about ten or fifteen minutes away. The problem is, while I think it is sweet that you want to help, you won't be able to touch someone's child without them thinking you are some kind of pervert."

"You're right," Joe said. "I hadn't considered that."

"I have an idea. Just follow my lead when we get there."

They drove to the children's hospital. When they got inside, Katie asked where they treated cancer patients. A cheerful volunteer directed them to an elevator and told them to take it to the second floor. When they got off the elevator, they found a room with a young girl lying in bed. She had a scarf around her head and looked to be around seven years old. Her parents were sitting in chairs next to her.

Katie walked in first and said, "Hi. We're from the Three Eagles Church of the Healer, and we would like to pray for you if you will let us."

The parents looked at each other, and then the woman said, "Sure. It couldn't hurt."

Katie introduced herself and Joe. The girl's parents stood up, and everyone shook hands. "I'm Jill, and this is my husband, Tim," the woman said.

"We are very pleased to meet you," Katie said. She then turned to the little girl. "What's your name, Honey?"

"Marie," the girl said, barely audible.

"Hello, Marie," Joe said. "I knew someone very special with that same name."

"You did? Where is she now?"

Joe pointed up and said, "She is looking down on us from Heaven."

"I'm sorry," Marie said.

"Don't be sorry," Joe said. "She lived a long and happy life, like you are going to do."

"What is wrong with Marie?" Katie asked the parents.

"She has a brain tumor," the mother said. "The doctors say they can't remove it, so they are treating her with chemotherapy and radiation."

Joe held Marie's hand and reached for Katie's. He said, "Let's all hold hands and pray silently." Katie reached out and held Tim's hand while he held Jill's hand. Jill then completed the circle by holding Marie's hand.

Joe connected with the little girl and quickly found the tumor. He worked on cutting off its blood supply. Without blood, it would die and slowly get absorbed and discarded as waste. After ten minutes, he let go of Marie's hand and said, "I feel very optimistic about your future, young lady."

She looked at Joe and asked, "Are you an angel?"

Joe put his finger to his lips and said, "That's our little secret."

Katie said, "It was a pleasure meeting you, and we wish you the best."

After they left the room, Katie asked, "What happened in there? Why did she ask if you are an angel?"

"I might have slipped and let her in a little."

"Oh, Joe. I know how much helping people means to you, but you can't let people know what you can do. You need more practice before you try that again."

"You're right, Katie. It is challenging to separate the mind from the brain while working so close to both."

"I have felt what you can do, Joe, but I have no clue how you are able to do it. I know it must be difficult, and I am proud of you even if you are not perfect yet. I wish I could help you, but the only thing I can do is let you practice on me."

"That is helping me, and I can't think of anyone I'd rather practice on," Joe said.

"What about the girl?" Katie asked. "Will she be okay?"

"The cancer won't be an issue for her anymore, although she will need to recover from all the poisons they put into her. I would need much more time to help her with that."

"You can only do what you can do. At least that little girl will have a chance at a long life now."

"Yes. I feel good about that."

Katie grabbed Joe's hand and squeezed. "Me too," she said. "I'm glad we came here."

***

When they returned to the car, Katie checked her phone and saw an email from Billy. She opened it and said, "Billy sent information on those people who were in Holly's room."

"I guess we'll be spending some time talking to them tomorrow," Joe said. "What time is Virginia's funeral?"

"It's at ten o'clock. We should have plenty of time in the afternoon."

"What about clothes? I was just wondering what we are going to wear?"

"Oh, shoot! I didn't think about that. We didn't bring anything appropriate for a funeral."

"I guess we need to find a store that sells funeral clothes," Joe said.

"Funeral clothes? Really? I'm pretty sure nobody calls it that."

"I do. I have two suits. One I wear to weddings, and the other I wear to funerals, and I've worn the funeral suit too many times these last twenty-five years."

"If you have a twenty-five-year-old suit, I think it's a good time to shop for a new one. I'm surprised it still fits you."

"Really? Do you think I've gained weight?"

"I guess that was a stupid thing to say. I forgot that you are always perfect."

"I'm far from perfect. If you are envious that I can maintain a good weight, you needn't be because I can help you with that, even though it has never been necessary for me to do so."

"I know you can, Joe. I'm not envious. It's just natural to outgrow your clothes, even as an adult. I guess I'm so comfortable with you now that I forget you are different."

"I hope you always forget I'm different. You said you wanted a normal life, and I want that, too. I don't want you to think of me as the guy who is different."

Katie put her hand on Joe's knee and said, "How about I think of you as the guy I love and the guy who makes me happy."

"That works for me," Joe said.

"Good," Katie said. "Now we have to figure out who sells funeral clothes."

Katie searched on her phone and found that there were very few stores selling both men's and women's clothes. They ended up at JCPenney, where

Katie helped Joe pick out a black suit and a white shirt. Joe tried on the suit and showed it to Katie.

"You look so handsome," she said, "but you need a tie." She found a display with ties and picked out a plain black tie. "Here, put this on."

"Joe put on the tie, and Katie said, "You will be the most handsome man at the funeral."

"Finally. My lifetime goal will be achieved."

"Don't be a smartass," Katie said.

When they reached the women's section, Katie found a black dress she wanted to try on. She returned wearing a very low-cut evening gown with a long slit up the left leg. Earlier, she had her long, dark hair tied behind her head, but now it hung naturally. Joe looked at her and said, "Wow! Are you going to a funeral or competing for Miss Wisconsin?"

"If I were competing for Miss Wisconsin, what do you think my chances would be?"

"I think all the other contestants would forfeit after seeing you."

"You sure do have a way with words. I'm going to buy this for you."

"I don't think it will look as good on me."

Katie laughed, shook her head, and said, "You know what I mean. I still need to find something for the funeral."

After trying on several outfits, Katie settled on a black pantsuit with a white blouse. They paid for their purchases and left the store.

***

On the way to the car, Katie said, "I want to call Gabe and see if he's learned anything about the list of suspects yet. There's no point in repeating what he's already done."

They got in the car, and Katie dialed Gabe's number. When it started ringing, she hit the speaker button. "Hello, Katie," Gabe said.

"Hi, Gabe. We were just wondering what you learned about the people who were in Holly's room?"

"So far, we've learned nothing useful. They all claim innocence, and I have no evidence pointing to any of them."

"Okay, thanks, Gabe. Please let us know if you learn anything new. Oh, and I hope your date night goes well."

"Thanks, Katie."

When Katie hung up, she started the engine and said, "It's almost six. Let's go talk to Dr. Rand."

Ten minutes later, they were sitting in Dr. Rand's office. "I was surprised to see you two again tonight," she said.

"We watched the autopsy tapes," Joe said.

"You did? Did you see something you don't understand? Is that why you're here?"

"We're here because we want to know why three of the bodies were already opened and restitched," Joe said.

Dr. Rand looked at them, confused, and said, "You didn't know?

"Know what?" Katie asked.

"Oh, I'm sorry," Dr. Rand said. "I thought you knew they were organ donors."

"Organ donors?" Katie said. "You mean someone took out body parts before they got to you?"

"That's right. It's not uncommon for me to see that, although three out of four is unusual."

"How can they take someone's organs before they know what the cause of death is?" Joe asked.

"In these particular cases, I imagine the autopsy was just a formality. I don't know what happened before I got them exactly, but their causes of death were probably pretty certain."

"How long must a person be dead before their organs are no longer any good for anybody?" Joe asked.

"It varies depending on the organ, but the sooner, the better. I would say that the organs must be removed within the first two hours after death or less."

"Who removes the organs?" Katie asked.

"I'm afraid that's something I'm not very familiar with, but I think there are surgeons trained in organ removals. When a donor is identified, a surgeon is called in to remove the organ and prep it for transportation, unless, of course, it is being donated to a person in the same hospital."

"Can you tell us where these bodies came from?" Joe asked.

"Sure, just a minute," Dr. Rand said. She tapped a few keys, looked at her screen, tapped a few more keys, and said, "Hmmm."

"What does 'hmmm' mean?" Katie asked.

"It says here that the same hospital transferred all three."

"Which hospital?" Katie asked.

"They all came from Jackson McCormick Hospital."

"The coincidences keep piling up," Joe said. "We need to examine the hospital more closely."

"I agree," Katie said before standing up. She held her hand out and shook Dr. Rand's hand. "Thank you so much for your time. You've been a big help."

***

When they left the coroner's office, Katie said, "I believe you are right. Dr. Rand looked surprised to see where the bodies came from. I don't think she is involved."

"Probably not, unless she is good at acting. So, what do you want to do now? Should we go out for dinner?"

Let's just get take-out tonight. I know a place that makes a good cheesesteak sandwich."

"Sounds good to me," Joe said before Katie took out her phone and called in their order.

They drove to the restaurant, picked up their order, and returned to the hotel. They put the food on a small table in their hotel room and ate. Katie said, "How will we figure out who killed Holly? I mean, Gabe investigated everyone on that list and came up empty."

"It's like putting together a puzzle. We need to find all the pieces and determine how they fit together. We don't have all the pieces yet. It takes time."

"And patience, which I have very little of," Katie said.

"Some investigations take years. We've only been at this for three days."

"We need to get moving then because I'm not spending years on this case."

"We can go home anytime you want to, Katie."

"I know, but I want to do this for Ashley."

"Do you want to do this for Ashley or for yourself?"

Katie sighed. "I mostly want to do it for Ashley, but I will admit that I also enjoy the challenge."

"I like that about you," Joe said. "I like that you are not content to accept things the way they are. It is that spunk I was talking about."

"I think we need to come up with a better word than spunk. How about awesomeness?"

Joe laughed and said, "Okay, awesomeness it is."

After eating, they sat on the bed together, and Katie opened her laptop. She checked her email and found what Billy sent her. "Okay, the first name on the list is Dr. Quincy Hoffman."

"Quincy? Who names their kid Quincy?"

"Who names their kid Josip?"

"Good point."

Anyway, he's an emergency room physician. He's thirty-five years old and has been with the hospital for eight years. He has a wife and two children and lives in the Fox Point area.

"Where's that?" Joe asked.

"It's a bit north of here, near the lake. Needless to say, it is where a doctor might live."

"What about the others?"

"There's Brennan Robertson, a nurse."

"A male nurse?"

"Yes, Joe. There are male nurses now. This isn't 1940."

"I know that. It proves that men can do anything women can do."

Katie looked at Joe, shook her head, and said, "Can I get back to the list, or do you have more smart-ass comments you want to make?"

"Carry on," Joe said.

"As I was saying, Brennan Robertson started working at Jackson McCormick Hospital around the same time Holly started. In fact, they went to nursing school together."

"Oh, so they were probably friends," Joe said.

"Maybe, but they might have also been competitors."

"What else does it say about him?"

"Well, he's thirty-three years old and has never been married. He lives not far from the hospital."

"Okay, who's next?"

"Next is Dr. Adam Mechs, the hospital administrator. He is fifty-two years old, married, and has three children, all over eighteen."

"He's somebody we need to talk to," Joe said.

"We need to talk to all of them, but not tonight."

Katie closed her laptop and set it on the nightstand. She turned off her light and leaned over to kiss Joe. He kissed her back and said, "I thought you were in a hurry to solve this case."

Katie climbed on top of Joe, kissed him again, and said, "I'm in a hurry for something much better than this case."

Chapter 10

Katie woke up the next morning and looked at the clock. "Oh, crap! It's almost eight. We've got to hurry up and get ready."

"Joe opened his eyes, looked at Katie, and said, "Relax. We have two hours."

"Have you learned nothing about women these last hundred years? Maybe you can get ready in five minutes, but it takes me time to look beautiful."

"Really? I think you look beautiful now."

"Ughhhh! Don't look at me," Katie said as she got out of bed. "My hair is a mess. I don't want you to see me like this."

Joe smiled and got out of bed as Katie headed to the shower. He opened the shower door to get in with her, but she held him back. "No! If you get in here, we'll end up having sex, and we don't have time for that. Why don't you make me a cup of coffee while you're waiting?"

Joe reluctantly left the shower and opened a package of coffee. He put the pod into the coffee maker, poured water into the machine, and turned the lever to the picture that showed one cup. He then turned on the power switch. As the coffee was brewing, he found little containers of coffee cream. He read the ingredients and thought Katie would need some healing after drinking her coffee.

After Joe took a shower, he put on his new suit. Katie stopped putting on her makeup and got up to examine him. She straightened his tie and said, "Wow! You look so handsome. Now, I regret not letting you have your way with me this morning."

"I hope you remember that next time."

Katie put her hand on Joe's cheek and said, "You're so cute."

When they were ready, they headed to Virginia's funeral service. It was held at the Catholic church that she and Henry attended. Katie had seen the church before, but never paid much attention to it. She thought it was smaller and less grandiose than other Catholic churches she had seen.

Once inside, they found Ashley, Henry, John, and the kids greeting people as they arrived. Everyone hugged, and an usher brought Katie and Joe to a second-row pew. Virginia's casket was on a pedestal in front of the altar. It was closed, which was a relief to Katie. She did not want her last memory of Virginia to be of her lying in a casket.

The inside of the church more than made up for the plainness of the outside. Beautiful stained glass windows lined the walls, each depicting a scene from the bible. The first window depicted Jesus's birth, and each window after that progressed through the New Testament, with the last window showing Jesus with his hands out, showing Thomas the holes from the crucifixion. Katie's parents were big on attending church, although they were Lutheran, not Catholic. Even so, this church had many similarities to the one she attended as a child.

While they waited, a woman played organ music. Gabe and his wife arrived and sat next to them. "Hi, Katie. Hi Joe," Gabe said. "You remember my wife, Carmen?"

"Of course," Katie said. "It is lovely to see you again."

Carmen was a beautiful middle-aged woman with lovely brown eyes and long, straight dark brown hair. She wore a modest black dress with long sleeves and a wide-brimmed black hat with a black flower on one side. "We should get together for something besides weddings and funerals," she said.

"That would be great," Katie said. "We would like that."

After about ten minutes, Ashley and her family sat in the first row. Ashley smiled at them as she took her seat. The church choir then sang an old hymn before the priest came out and asked everyone to stand for a prayer. A few days before, the same priest had given Ashley last rites.

The priest then gave a fairly long sermon about tragedies, free will, and the healing power of God's love. He then talked about Virginia. "Our beloved Virginia, wife of Henry, mother of Ashley, has gone to be with the Lord. But this tragedy has brought us proof that God is watching and he does care. Less than five days ago, Virginia's daughter, Ashley Taylor, was at Heaven's Gate. The doctors had given up. I was asked to give her last rites, which I did, but God decided that she had more work to do here on Earth, so he sent an angel to heal her."

Katie looked at Joe and smiled. She had not gone to church since she left home and wasn't even sure if God existed. Now, she wondered if God did exist. Maybe he had something to do with Joe's abilities. She had heard stories of angels mating with humans. Perhaps the first healer resulted from an angel and a human having a child. Maybe God encouraged Joe's mother to leave the war zone and come to America to preserve the good that had been created. Then she thought how crazy that sounded. She probably subconsciously wanted Joe to be an actual angel.

The priest continued, "Ashley sits here today, alive and well, due to God's power and mercy."

Someone clapped, and soon everyone was clapping. The priest held up his hands, and the crowd quieted. "We are here today to remember and honor the life of Virginia Hall, but we are also here to honor God for proving with actions, time and again, that he loves us always. Now, may the peace of God, which surpasses all understanding, keep your hearts and minds in Christ Jesus. Let us pray."

When the service ended, everyone filed out, hugging Ashley and her family again before leaving. When Katie and Joe reached her, she asked them to wait. Once all the guests had left the church, Ashley walked outside with them. "I heard you found Mom's killer. That was fast. Will you be heading home now?"

"No. Not yet. Someone murdered your mom's killer, and we want to find out who did it and why," Katie said.

"I didn't hear about that. It's probably not very Christian to say this in front of a church, but I can't say that I'm sad about her death."

"We think your mom stumbled onto a conspiracy, and we would like to solve it for her."

Ashley reached out and held Katie's and Joe's hands. "I was wrong when I said Joe was an angel. I should have said you are both angels. We are having a private ceremony at the gravesite in about an hour. After that, I will be free. Please let me know if I can help you in any way."

"We will," Katie said. They hugged again before leaving.

***

When Katie and Joe left the service, Joe said, "I'd like to return to the hotel and get out of this monkey suit."

"It's not a monkey suit. I think you look very handsome."

"I'm sorry, Katie, but I'm not like you. I prefer to feel comfortable."

"What are you talking about? I like to be comfortable."

"Maybe, but you like looking fancy even more. You love getting dressed up and putting those high heels on. Frankly, I don't know how any woman can wear those things."

"I like looking 'fancy,' as you call it, because I want you to be attracted to me. You should appreciate that instead of giving me a hard time about it."

"Are we fighting right now?" Joe asked. "I don't want to be one of those couples that fight."

"I don't either, so tell me you're sorry."

Joe was about to say the same to Katie, but changed his mind. "I'm sorry. I appreciate that you want to look good for me, but you should know I am attracted to you, not your clothes."

Katie kissed Joe and said, "I'm attracted to you, too. It's just nice to see you dressed up sometimes."

"Okay, how about this? We will dress up for a fancy date night once or twice a month."

"I would love that, Joe."

They returned to the hotel, put on casual clothes, and then went out for lunch. After lunch, they headed to the hospital to talk to the people who were in Holly's room the day she was murdered.

When they arrived at the hospital, they went to the information desk. Katie said, "Hi. My name is Katie, and this is Joe. We are from Channel 23 News. We would like to speak with Dr. Quincy Hoffman."

The woman behind the desk said, "Just a minute." She picked up her phone, dialed a number, and after a few seconds said, "This is Karen at information. A couple of news reporters are here asking to speak with Dr. Hoffman." There was a thirty-second pause before the woman said, "Okay," and hung up the phone. She looked at Katie, pointed to her left, and said, "Take the elevator to the third floor. He'll meet you there."

A doctor was there waiting for them when they got off the elevator. He was young, perhaps thirty, with a handsome face and sandy blonde hair. Katie thought he looked more like a doctor on a soap opera show, not that she would watch that kind of show, except once in a while when she was bored, which hadn't happened since she met Joe. "Hi. You must be Dr. Hoffman." Katie said, holding out her hand.

They shook hands, and Dr. Hoffman pointed at his nametag and said, "That's me."

"Of course. I'm Katie, and this is, uh, Joe. We are with Channel 23 News. We'd like to talk to you about Holly Johnson."

"Oh, yes. That was a shame about her. I assume I am on your suspect list."

"It's more like a possible suspect list," Katie said.

"Follow me," the doctor said, leading them to an empty patient room. "Okay, ask me anything."

"You were the doctor treating Holly Johnson. Is that correct?" Katie asked.

"Yes. That's right."

"What was her condition when you last saw her?"

"She was alive and well, if that's what you mean."

"What about her physical condition?" Joe asked.

"Besides a few bruises, I couldn't find anything wrong with her. She didn't have a head injury, so I couldn't understand why she was unconscious. I figured she had some kind of mental breakdown."

"Why didn't you hook up a monitoring device to her?" Joe asked.

"I didn't feel it was necessary. Those machines are used mostly to alert the staff if a patient suffers a traumatic event. In Holly Johnson's case, I didn't think that would happen. If someone hadn't killed her, she would have been fine."

"If you had used a monitor, someone would have been alerted to her murder," Joe said.

"Are you suggesting I didn't use a monitor to cover up a murder?"

"Nobody is suggesting anything, Dr. Hoffman," Katie said while looking sternly at Joe. "We are just trying to learn the truth."

"The truth is, I don't know what happened. I only know she was fine when I left."

"Did you know Holly Johnson when she worked here?" Joe asked.

"Yes. I knew her. I didn't know her well. I mean, we weren't friends or anything."

"So you never had sexual relations with her?"

Katie gave Joe another stern look.

"No. Of course not. I'm married."

"I didn't ask if you were married."

"I'm happily married."

"Okay, Doctor," Katie said. "We appreciate your time. We'll let you know if we have any more questions."

When they left the room, Katie said, "What was that all about?"

"I was just trying to get the truth out of him."

"It sounded to me like you decided not to like the guy for some reason."

"It sounded to me like you decided to like him for some reason. You were so enamored by him, you couldn't remember my name."

Katie looked at Joe momentarily and said, "You're jealous."

"Jealous of him? That's ridiculous. I'm not jealous."

Katie smiled and said, "Yes, you are. Okay, I admit, I did find him attractive, but he's an eight at best. You're a ten. I wouldn't trade you for him even if he were a fifteen."

"Okay, I accept your apology," Joe said.

Katie laughed and kissed Joe on the cheek. She said, "I am the luckiest woman on Earth. You never have to worry about me."

"I know that. I'm the luckiest man on Earth, too."

"So let's go talk to our next victim, I mean suspect."

They went to the nurses' station and asked where they could find Brennan Robertson. The woman behind the counter looked at her computer and said he was off but would be in the following morning.

"What about Dr. Adam Mechs?"

"The hospital administrator? I don't have his schedule. The administrative offices are on the seventh floor. I suggest asking someone up there."

"Okay. Thanks for your help," Katie said.

They took the elevator to the seventh floor. It opened to a hallway with a window overlooking the parking lot. They went left and saw several empty offices. One office had a middle-aged woman working at her desk. They opened her door, and Katie said, "Hi. We are with Channel 23 News. We're looking for Dr. Mechs."

"I'm afraid he won't be in until Monday. Can I leave a message for him?"

"No, thank you," Katie said. "We'll come back."

They left the room, and Katie asked, "Now what?"

"Did Billy give you their home addresses?"

"Yes, he did. That's a good idea. Let's go bother them at their homes."

When they reached Katie's car, Joe asked, "Who should we talk to first?"

"Brennan Robertson is not far from here. Let's talk to him first. Please be nice to him, even if he's good-looking."

"Just because I ask uncomfortable questions sometimes doesn't mean I'm not being nice."

"It kind of does. I'm not saying we should throw softballs at them, but we should start subtle and hit them with tough questions if they are being uncooperative."

"Okay. I'll follow your lead."

***

They parked on the street in front of Robertson's house. It was an older, two-story home with similar homes crowded next to it. There were barely eight feet between houses. They climbed the stairs, and Katie pushed the doorbell button, but heard nothing. She waited thirty seconds and then knocked on the door. After another thirty seconds, a man answered the door. He was tall and slim with medium-length dark hair. He wore blue jeans and a T-shirt that seemed tight on him. "Hello. Can I help you?"

"Yes. I'm Katie, and this is Joe. We are with Channel 23 News. Are you Brennan Robertson?"

"Yes. What is this about?"

"Can we speak with you about Holly Johnson?"

"He looked back into his house, stepped outside, and closed the door."

"What do you want to know?" he said.

"We learned that you went to school with her and started working at the hospital around the same time she did. Is that correct?" Katie asked.

"Yes. That's right."

"So I assume you knew her well. Did you like her?" Katie asked.

"Of course. We were very close."

"How close? Joe asked. "Were you intimate?"

Katie kicked Joe in the shin and said, "We are just trying to establish what kind of relationship you two had."

He looked at Joe and said, "We were not intimate in the way you are talking about. She's not my type."

"What is your type?" Joe asked.

Robertson looked at him and said, "Wouldn't you like to know?"

"You saw Holly the day she died. Why were you in her room?" Katie asked.

"I told you we were close. I went in there to see her. I told her I missed her and said that if she woke up, I would never let so much time pass again without seeing her."

"Did you examine her while you were in there?" Katie asked.

"No. I wasn't there as a nurse. I was there as her friend. I just held her hand. I wanted her to know I was there."

"Did her hand feel cold?" Joe asked.

"A little cool. I figured she had poor circulation due to the accident. Wait a minute. Do you think she was dead already when I went in there? Oh, God. I held her hand and didn't even notice."

"We don't know exactly when she died," Katie said. "That's what we are trying to find out. So think. Was that a dead hand you were holding?"

A tear formed in the corner of his eye. He shook his head and said, "I just don't know."

Katie handed him a business card and said, "Thank you for your time. This is my number. Please call if you think of anything."

When they returned to the car, Joe said, "Why did you kick me in there?"

"Because the man was obviously gay. I didn't want you to embarrass yourself by asking if he slept with Holly."

"He's gay? Really? How do you know?"

"I know you've been secluded in your cabin for the last twenty years, but sometimes you act like you just woke up from a fifty-year snooze."

"That's ridiculous. I may not be as hep as you, but I'm not that bad."

"Hep?"

"Hip. I mean hip."

Katie put her hand on Joe's knee. "Just stick with me. I'll let you know when you act like Rip Van Winkle."

"Thanks a lot."

Chapter 11

Dr. Adam Mechs lived in a high-rise condo building near downtown that overlooked Lake Michigan. Katie and Joe took the elevator to the seventeenth floor. Katie knocked on the door, and they waited. The door opened, and a woman answered. She looked to be in her late forties and in great shape. She was wearing yoga pants and a tank top. Sweat beaded from her forehead like she had been working out inside the condo unit. "Can I help you?" she asked.

"Hi. I'm Katie, and this is Joe. We are with Chanel 23 News. We are looking to speak with Dr. Mechs."

"What is this about?"

"We are investigating the deaths of Virginia Hall and Holly Johnson. We thought he might be able to help us."

"Just a moment," she said and closed the door. After about a minute, Dr. Mechs opened the door. He also looked like he had been working out. He wore a T-shirt and athletic shorts. He had a towel in one hand. "My wife says you are reporters. What can I do for you?"

"We are from Channel 23 News," Katie said. "I'm Katie, and this is Joe. I hope we didn't come at a bad time."

"It's fine. We just finished our workout."

"We want to talk to you about Holly Johnson and Virginia Hall."

"I know about Holly, but don't know who Virginia Hall is."

"Virginia is the mother of Ashley Taylor."

Dr. Mechs thought for a moment and said, "Oh, yes. The miracle woman." He opened the door wider and said, "Please, come in."

They walked inside, and the doctor closed the door behind them. Straight ahead was a large window with a beautiful view of the lake. A treadmill and a stationary bike stood in front of the window. To the left was a kitchen and dining room, and to the right was a living room with a beautiful tan leather sectional sofa.

"Your place is lovely," Katie said.

"Thank you," Dr. Mechs said, who had moved beside his wife. "This is my wife, Helen."

They all shook hands, and Helen said, "Won't you sit down?"

Katie and Joe sat at one end of the sofa while Dr. Mechs and his wife sat at the other. "Can I get you folks something to drink?" Helen asked.

"No, thank you," Katie and Joe said in unison.

"We'd like to ask you about Holly Johnson," Joe said.

"Oh, yes. I was shocked when I learned someone had killed her in my hospital."

"You were in her room around the time of her death. Why were you there?" Joe asked.

"She had been a nurse at our hospital for several years. When I learned she was at the hospital as a patient, I felt obligated to pay her a visit. I didn't stay long. I checked her chart and then told her that we missed her at the hospital and hoped she would recover soon."

"Did you examine her while you were there?" Katie asked. "Did you hold her hand or anything like that?"

"No. I did none of that. I wasn't her physician, and I don't go around touching other women." He looked at his wife, who smiled.

"So, you don't know for sure if she was alive when you saw her?" Joe asked.

"What? Do you think she was already dead when I saw her?"

"We don't know," Joe said. "We are trying to determine when she died."

"Dr. Mechs thought momentarily and said, "I just don't know. I assumed she was unconscious. I was not paying attention to her breathing. Now I feel terrible. I should have noticed that."

"Dr. Mechs. I assume your hospital performs organ transplants. Is that correct?" Katie asked.

"Yes, of course. We have surgeons who specialize in transplants. We have a great success rate in that area."

"What about lately? Have you secured more organs than usual these last few months?"

Dr. Mechs thought about it and said, "Now that you mention it, it seems like our patients have waited less time than usual lately, but we seem to go through periods of feast or famine."

"Let me ask you a hypothetical question," Joe said. "If a potential organ donor died nearby and a surgeon at your hospital was tasked with removing the organ, who would most likely get that organ if a patient at your hospital needed it and another patient in Chicago also needed it?"

"There is an independent review board that determines that, but if the patients were equal, I would say the closer patient would get it. If the patient in Chicago had a better chance of long-term survival, then that patient would get it, assuming it could be delivered within the required window. What does this have to do with Holly Johnson or Virginia, uh, what was her name?"

"Virginia Hall," Katie said. "We believe the hospital is benefiting from the murder of homeless people," Katie said.

"What?" Helen blurted out. "That can't be true."

"It's okay, Dear," Dr. Mechs said. "I'm sure there is a misunderstanding here." He turned to Katie and Joe and said, "I don't know what is happening here, but if you think the hospital is getting rich from transplants, I can assure you that is not the case. In fact, transplants are one of the least profitable procedures done at our hospital. The time and resources involved are high. We do them to save people who would normally die otherwise. The biggest benefit to the hospital would be the satisfaction of sending someone home instead of to the morgue."

"Do you recall the name Olivia Park?" Joe asked. "She was an organ donor? Her organs were removed at your hospital. Do you know if a patient in your hospital received them?"

Dr. Mechs thought momentarily and said, "Yes, I do remember her. I believe her heart and eyes were sent to patients in other hospitals, but we did have a patient in our hospital who received her liver."

"Can you tell us who the patient was?" Joe asked.

"I don't remember. Even if I did, I'm afraid I can't legally divulge that information."

"What about the doctor who performed the surgery?"

"I can tell you that. The surgeon was Dr. Christine Hart. She is a specialist in transplant surgery."

"Okay, Doctor. I think we have taken enough of your time. We appreciate you talking to us," Katie said.

"Well, good luck with your investigation. I think you're wrong about people getting killed for body parts, but if you're right, I hope you catch whoever is responsible. I also hope you find whoever killed Holly Johnson."

As they headed down the elevator, Katie asked, "Okay, Joe, who do you think is lying?"

"I have to admit that I have no idea."

"You have no idea? You told me you were good at reading people."

"I also said I wasn't an expert. In this case, I'm either not as good as I thought, or the killer is an exceptional liar. Remember, too, that there may have been more people in Holly's room than was reported."

"That's true, so all these people could be innocent. That leaves us with nothing to go on."

"We hit a dead end on the last case and got through it."

"Yes, we did, but that was then. This is now," Katie said. "We have no suspects, and now it seems our motive has gone out the window."

The elevator door opened, and Katie and Joe walked out and headed toward the car. "I don't think we lost the motive entirely. If Dr. Mechs wasn't lying, then the financial incentive for the hospital doesn't exist, but what about the doctor? There's also the possibility that the victims' families are paying for these organs under the table, even if the distribution is totally legal. Maybe if the family pays up, a body suddenly becomes available."

"That's possible, but it seems a bit unlikely," Katie said as she unlocked the car and got in.

Joe got in, closed the door, and put his seatbelt on. "Yeah, I suppose it is."

"Let's go back to the hospital and see if Dr. Hart is working today," Katie said.

***

Katie couldn't find a parking spot near the hospital's main entrance, so she parked near the emergency room. A large white Cadillac pulled up to the emergency entrance as they walked toward the building. A woman, perhaps in her early seventies, got out of the car. She was nearly hysterical. When she saw Katie and Joe, she said, "Please help! My husband's having a heart attack."

Joe opened the passenger door and saw a man who looked to be around seventy-five. He was thin and held his right hand over his chest. He was breathing hard. Joe grabbed his arm and helped him out of the car. Katie got on the other side of him, and they helped him walk into the emergency room. Once inside, his wife yelled to anyone who would listen that her husband was having a heart attack.

Thirty seconds later, someone showed up with a wheelchair and helped him sit down. Joe said to the man, "Don't worry. Your heart is fine. You are having a bad case of acid reflux."

Joe didn't wait for a reply. He just grabbed Katie's hand, and they walked away. "I hadn't thought of it before, but you can help people by diagnosing what's wrong with them," Katie said. "Maybe you can get a job in a doctor's office."

"I would need a medical license for that. I don't think I want to go to school for years to learn something I will never use."

"You have a point. I don't know. Maybe you can become a massage therapist or something like that."

"That would be more realistic, but I don't think I would encounter too many people who need the kind of help I could give."

They reached the information desk, and Katie said, "Hi. We're from Channel 23 News. We would like to speak with Dr. Christine Hart if she's available."

The woman behind the desk tapped a few keys and said, "I'm sorry, but she's in surgery."

"Do you know when she'll be done?" Katie asked.

"She is scheduled for two hours, which, of course, is just an estimate. She is currently at one hour and forty-five minutes, so she may be available soon. If you want to wait, the surgery department is on this floor. Just go past the elevators and follow the signs."

"Okay, great. Thank you so much," Katie said.

They followed the signs to the surgery department. The waiting room was empty except for a middle-aged man sitting in one of the chairs. Katie and Joe sat down several chairs away from him.

"Good afternoon," The man said. "Do you folks have a loved one in surgery?"

"No. We are just here to talk to the doctor."

"Oh, that's good. My wife is having her gallbladder removed."

"That's too bad," Katie said. "I hope she'll be okay."

"That is too bad," Joe whispered. "I could have fixed her."

Katie nudged Joe on the side, and the man said. "The doctor says it's no big deal."

"It is a big deal," Joe whispered before Katie nudged him again.

"That's good to know," Katie said.

The doctor came out and spared them from further awkward conversation. She was about forty, a little shorter than average, with short, straight, ash blonde hair. She said, "Mr. Conner. The surgery went well, and your wife will be fine."

"She won't be fine," Joe said, getting a dirty look from Katie.

"I just can't take you anywhere."

When the doctor was finished talking to the man, Katie and Joe approached her. Katie said, "Hi. I'm Katie, and this is Joe. We are with Channel 23 News. Are you Dr. Christine Hart?"

"Yes, I am. What can I do for you?"

"We'd like to ask you a few questions," Katie said.

"What is this about?"

"Why do you tell your patients that removing their gallbladder is no big deal?" Joe asked. "Do you even know what the gallbladder does?"

"Of course, I know what the gallbladder does. Is that why you're here? Are you doing some kind of hit piece on me?"

Katie pinched Joe hard on the arm. "I'm sorry about my partner. He can be passionate at times, but that is not why we are here."

"So you know, I never said removing the gallbladder was no big deal. I might have said something like the surgery was no big deal. I try to put my patients at ease."

"Do you ever offer your patients an alternative to surgery?" Joe asked.

"By the time they come to me, they have already gone through all their alternatives with their primary doctor. Now, why are you here?"

"We have questions about transplant surgeries," Katie said. "We were told that you are a transplant specialist. If that's true, why are you doing simple surgeries like gallbladders?"

"If I only did transplants, I wouldn't make enough money to pay my insurance."

"Are you saying transplant surgery doesn't pay well?" Joe asked.

"No, I'm not saying that. It pays pretty well, but I only do about four or five monthly."

"Have you done more than average these last few months?" Katie asked.

Dr. Hart thought for a moment and said, "Yes. Now that you mention it, it does seem like the numbers have increased lately. What is this about, anyway?"

"We are investigating the deaths of several homeless people that seem connected to organ donations."

"Are you serious?" Dr. Hart asked. "Do you think someone is murdering people for body parts?"

"That's what we are trying to find out," Katie said.

"Why homeless people?" Dr. Hart asked.

"There are probably a few reasons," Joe said. "We believe our killer sees the lives of homeless people to be less valuable than the lives of others. I would also guess a significant reason is that most homeless people do not have a family support group that will push for an investigation into their deaths."

"If someone were murdering people for body parts, how would they ensure that the body part goes to the correct patient?" Katie asked.

"The only way to ensure that is to not only have a criminal doctor, but you would also need at least one medically trained person to assist, plus an anesthesiologist. In addition, you would have to have a private place to do surgery. After that, you would have to dispose of the body where nobody would find it and possibly figure out what you are doing."

"That seems complicated," Joe said.

"I haven't even mentioned that the patient's family would have to keep quiet, and the fact that the patient suddenly recovered would need to be explained. That person would need to take anti-rejection medication. How would they get that, or even explain why they need it?"

"The victims in question had correctly gone through the system," Katie said. "Their organs were removed by someone at this hospital, presumably you, and then transplanted into patients here," Katie said. "In a case like that, how can one be assured of getting an organ?"

"I don't think they can," Dr. Hart said, "However, if I were involved, which I'm not, of course, I would find a victim similar to my patient. I would want someone about the same size, the same sex, and with the same blood type. It would also help if I had someone on my side on the select committee."

"Who is on the select committee?" Katie asked.

"It contains a variety of people from different specialties, such as surgeons, psychiatrists, nurses, and I don't remember who else. I learned all about it in school but haven't paid too much attention to that end of the operation since then."

"Do you know who is on this committee?" Joe asked.

"Sorry. I can't help you there."

Katie handed Dr. Hart her business card and said, "If you can think of anything else that might help, please let us know."

"Of course," Dr. Hart said."

"Thank you so much."

They all shook hands, and Joe said, "I'm sorry if I gave you a hard time earlier. We appreciate your help."

When they left the room, Katie said, "What was that all about in there?"

"I'm sorry. I don't like doctors who remove body parts willy-nilly."

"Listen, Joe. I love that you are concerned for other people's welfare, but you can't save the world. We mere mortals have flaws. Many of these doctors are confident that their ways are right. Just because they don't know what you know doesn't make them bad people. Don't forget it was doctors who kept you alive long enough for you to save yourself after the explosion. You spent all your energy helping me, and it was the doctors who helped you."

"I know. You're right. I don't think doctors are bad people. I just hate to see people suffer unnecessarily."

"Nobody wants to see people suffer. Well, almost nobody. It would be best to focus on the people you can help and stop worrying about people you can do nothing for. It is a burden that you don't need."

"You are right, Katie, as usual."

***

When Katie and Joe left the hospital, they decided to invite Gabe and Carmen to dinner. Katie dialed Gabe's number, said they were heading to an Italian restaurant, and asked if they wanted to join them. Gabe spoke with his wife, who agreed that that was a good idea.

They met Gabe and Carmen at an Italian restaurant near downtown. Katie had taken Joe to the same restaurant shortly after they met. Gabe and Carmen had also ditched their dressy attire for something more casual. After they were seated, Gabe said, "It is nice that we had a chance to get together like this."

"I agree," Katie said. "We needed a break from this investigation."

"Gabe tells me you two helped to catch Virginia Hall's killer," Carmen said.

"Yes, but now we are investigating who killed the killer," Katie said.

"Honey, it sounds like they want to take a break from the case," Gabe said.

"Oh, yes. I'm sorry."

"There's no need to be sorry," Katie said. "We don't mind talking about it. We just don't want to bore you by talking shop."

"Don't worry about that," Carmen said. "I think Gabe's work can be quite fascinating sometimes. Like finding a killer and then having the killer get murdered, just like Lee Harvey Oswald."

"A little different," Joe said. "Lee Harvey Oswald was shot on live television."

"Can you imagine being alive at that time and watching all that go down?" Gabe said.

"It was a very troubling time," Joe said. "I mean, it must have been."

"It's too bad we didn't catch our killer on camera," Katie said.

"Did anybody check for cameras at the hospital?" Joe asked.

I did," Gabe said. "There were none near Holly's room."

A young man came to their table and said, "Good evening. I'm Antonio. I'll be your server this evening."

He looked at Joe and said, "Oh, yes. You're the orange juice guy."

"That's me," Joe said.

"Orange juice guy?" Gabe asked.

"Joe likes orange juice," Katie said. "I joked that he couldn't get orange juice here, but then found out they have it."

"Would you like an orange juice?" Antonio asked.

"No. Not today. Can you bring us a bottle of Pinot Grigio?" He looked at Gabe and Carmen and said, "Our treat today."

When Antonio left, Carmen asked, "So, do you have any clues about who might have done it?"

"No, but we think we know why," Katie said.

Gabe looked at his wife and said, "I told you they were good. I wanted them to join the police force, but they decided to stay with the resort."

"So why was she murdered?" Carmen asked.

"We believe Holly Johnson was part of a conspiracy to murder homeless people for body parts," Katie said.

"That's terrible," Carmen said.

"Have you figured out how that would work?" Gabe asked.

"Sort of," Katie said. "Holly worked at Social Services, so she had access to the records of everyone who came there for help. If someone at Holly's former hospital needed a transplant, she could locate a person who was a close match. If she found a person who was the right size and sex with the same blood type, she would kill them in a way that made them an easy candidate for organ removal."

"How would they guarantee that their patient would get the organ and not someone in another hospital?" Gabe asked.

"They played the odds," Joe said. "By making sure their victim was a close match to their patient and by making sure the victim died close to their hospital, it was an easy choice for the selection committee. It also helps if they have someone on the transplant selection committee who is part of the conspiracy. Speaking of that, Gabe, do you think you can get a list of names of the people on that selection committee?

"Sure. I'll look into it."

I don't understand why a person would trade one life for another." Carmen said. "It seems pretty cold-blooded."

"It sure does," Katie said. "We think it is because her father died while waiting for a heart transplant. She might have decided that some lives are more valuable than others.

"So she was essentially playing God," Carmen said. "I guess God didn't like that."

"Or someone didn't like that she got herself caught," Joe said. "She probably threatened to tell the police everything if her partner didn't help her escape. The partner then decided that killing her was easier and left no possibility that she would ever talk to anyone."

The waiter arrived with their wine and poured everyone a glass. He then went over the specials and took everyone's order. When he left, the conversation shifted to other topics. They discussed the ski resort, Katie's new job as marketing manager, and Carmen's jewelry designs.

LAST RITES

They stayed for quite a while talking. When they finally left, it was late. Katie and Joe returned to their hotel room, showered together, and went straight to bed.

Chapter 12

Katie awoke the following morning to an empty bed. The sun had not yet risen, but an early morning light shone through the window around the closed curtain. "Joe? Joe? Are you here?"

She sat up in bed, turned on the light, and looked around. "Joe?"

After hearing no response, she got up and checked the bathroom, but it was empty. She opened her suitcase, took out some clothes, and dressed quickly. She opened the door and saw Joe approaching. He had a coffee in his hand. "Oh, you're up," he said, handing her the coffee.

They went back into the room, and Katie said, "You went downstairs to get me coffee? Why didn't you just make it in the room?"

"Well, I know you like cream in your coffee, but we only have that artificial cream up here, so I thought I would go down and get you the good stuff."

Katie kissed Joe and said, "Thank you. You are such a good husband. Next time, tell me before you leave. I was worried something happened to you."

"I'm sorry. I thought I would return before you woke up."

"I guess I've grown so accustomed to you being with me that I know when you're gone, even when I'm asleep."

"The human subconscious can be a powerful asset. I once told you that your healing was unconscious, and my healing was conscious. That is not entirely true. I have been healing myself for so long that I don't have to think about it. When I'm hurt, my subconscious mind knows what to do. That's why I can heal when I'm sleeping."

"So I guess my subconscious knows stuff, too. That means you can't sneak out on me in the middle of the night."

"Sneak out on you? Why in the world would I want to do that?"

"I don't know. Sometimes men get bored with their women."

"I think you are overgeneralizing men. Sometimes relationships end due to failures, which are most often caused by both partners."

"How would you know?" Katie asked. "You were with the same woman for over sixty years."

"I know because I have had friends and family members go through divorces and relationship problems. The fact that I lasted so long in one relationship should put you at ease."

Katie put her coffee down and hugged Joe. She kissed him and said, "I don't believe that you would ever do anything to hurt me. It's just that I feel like I've become addicted to you. If I ever lost you, I don't think I could handle the withdrawal."

"I know exactly how you feel, my dear. When you were hurt, I was afraid you might be dead. I don't think I had ever been so scared in my life, and I've had a long life."

They kissed again, this time passionately. The clothes that Katie had just put on came off again, and they ended up back in bed.

They were eating breakfast at the hotel restaurant two hours later when Katie's phone rang. She looked at the screen and saw that Gabe was calling. She answered it and put it on speaker. "Good morning, Gabe."

"Good morning, Katie. Is Joe there with you?"

"He's right here. What's going on?"

"I thought you two would like to know that the hospital administrator, Dr. Adam Mechs, is on the selection committee."

"That's interesting," Joe said. "So he could be part of this."

"He could be," Gabe said, "but being on the selection committee doesn't prove guilt."

"No, but it gives us something to think about," Joe said.

"Thanks for letting us know," Katie said.

"Certainly. Let me know if you learn anything."

"Of course. Thanks again, Gabe." Katie said.

When Katie hung up, she asked, "So what do we do now?"

"I have no idea. If Dr. Mechs is guilty, how can we prove it?"

"I don't know. Perhaps we should take a break and clear our heads."

"That's a good idea. What would you like to do?" Joe asked.

"Why don't we walk to the lake like we did the other day? This time, we can take a different route that will bring us past the shopping district."

"You want to go shopping?"

"Seriously, Joe. Have you met me?"

"Okay, but remember, we have to carry anything we buy."

"That's not exactly true. Anything I buy, you have to carry," Katie said, smiling.

"Wonderful," Joe said. "We should look for stores that sell small things."

"You mean like jewelry? I couldn't agree more."

After breakfast, they returned to their room to get their jackets. Katie took off her designer boots and put on a pair of sneakers.

When they left the hotel, they crossed the street, walked to the next block, and turned toward the lake. The street was like an outdoor shopping mall. There were a variety of high-end retail stores. Joe saw a clothing store, a shoe store, a jewelry store, a coffee shop, and a French restaurant, all within a stone's throw of where they were walking. "Let's go in here," Katie said as they passed the shoe store.

"Do you really need another pair of shoes?" Joe asked.

"Women don't buy shoes because they need them. I would think you would have learned that by now."

"When it comes to women, I gave up trying to learn long ago."

Katie slapped Joe on the arm and said, "You're so funny. You should be happy to know I am not here to buy myself a pair of shoes."

"You're not. So why are we here then?"

"We're here to buy you a pair of shoes."

"Me? I don't need shoes."

"Of course you do. You've had that same ratty old pair of sneakers since I met you."

Joe looked down at his shoes. "But I like these. They're comfortable."

"They're ugly. I'm almost embarrassed to be seen with you when you have those on."

Joe looked down at his feet again and said, "Okay, fine. I'll buy another pair if it will make you happy."

"Good," Katie said before flagging down a salesperson. "We have a shoe emergency here."

A young saleswoman looked at Joe's shoes and said, "You got here just in time."

"I'm surrounded by comedians," Joe said.

The woman measured Joe's feet and showed them several options for his size. Katie picked out a pair of blue and white New Balance sneakers that Joe tried on. He found them to be comfortable, so Katie told him to keep them on and asked the salesperson to dispose of Joe's old shoes.

After they paid for the shoes, they left the store and continued walking. "Don't you feel better now?" Katie asked.

"Of course. It feels good knowing that I am no longer embarrassing you."

"I think I said you 'almost' embarrassed me. Now you can rest easy for the next three months."

"Three months? Is that how often you replace your shoes?"

"No, but I change my shoes. You wear the same ones every day."

"Okay, fine. If it makes you happy to see me in new shoes, I will replace them whenever you think it's time."

"Good. Now, I'm sure it will make you happy to see me with a new purse. "Katie took Joe's hand and led him into a store that sold purses. She found a purse she liked and put it over her shoulder. "What do you think of this one?"

"I think it looks fantastic."

Katie studied Joe's face and said, "You don't care, do you?"

"Honestly, Katie, you could carry your stuff in a paper bag, and I'd love you just as much."

"I guess I shouldn't expect you to understand. I know you don't like shopping, and I love that you are putting up with this without complaining. Why don't we find a store that you want to look in? I'm pretty sure there is a camera store on the next block."

"Well, if you insist," Joe said.

They visited several more stores as they walked down the street. Katie decided that if she found something she liked, she would buy it on the way back so Joe wouldn't have to carry it so far. When they reached the camera store, Katie waited while Joe shopped. He found a camera that took 360-degree photos. He turned to Katie and said, "This might be something we can use to market the resort."

"Oh, yes. That would be fantastic. You should get it."

Joe looked at Katie and said, "You don't care, do you?"

They both laughed, and Joe said, "Okay. We'll pick it up on the way back."

They continued their walk until they reached the lake. They sat on a bench and just admired the view. After a while, Katie said, "I think we should head back and get some lunch. I'm getting hungry."

"I agree," Joe said, and they started walking back.

They hadn't walked very far when Joe noticed a blue sedan making a U-turn ahead of them. As the car approached, it slowed, and the passenger window rolled down. Joe thought the driver was going to stop and ask for directions. When the car got close, Joe looked inside and saw the driver was wearing a ski mask and pointing a handgun at them. He quickly turned toward Katie, put his arms around her, and picked her up. He carried her away from the car as quickly as possible.

The driver got off five shots and quickly drove away. The first three shots missed, but the fourth shot nicked Joe's left arm. The fifth shot hit him in the back. The force of the bullet pushed him off balance, and he fell forward. It all seemed to happen in slow motion for Joe. As he fell, he twisted his body to the right so he would not land on top of Katie. His right shoulder hit the grass hard. He tried to cushion Katie's fall but was only mildly successful.

Katie quickly got to her knees and checked on Joe. He was having trouble breathing. "Joe! Oh, my God!" She looked around and saw no one except a young woman about fifty yards away. She was jogging but stopped when she heard the gunshots. Katie yelled to her, "Help! We need help!"

The woman ran toward them, and when she got close, Katie said, "He's been shot. Call 911!"

Joe could feel that the bullet had hit one of his ribs and had broken apart. The pieces entered his right lung. He knew he needed to fix the problem quickly, but getting enough air was taking most of his concentration. He didn't think he could do it without help. He grabbed Katie's hand and concentrated. She was his only hope.

Chapter 13

When Joe connected with Katie, it surprised her at first. She could feel Joe's injuries. She knew he was having trouble getting enough air, but her lungs were working fine, so she wasn't burdened the same way Joe was. Normally, when Joe connected with her, she could feel Joe's internal organs as well as her own. She knew everything there was to know about Joe physically, but she could not feel his thoughts or emotions.

Nevertheless, she somehow knew what he wanted her to do. She needed to be the healer. She felt Joe's healing powers many times. She had no words for how it worked, but she knew it on a level beyond understanding. It was like knowing how to walk without knowing all the processes that make walking possible.

Katie reached behind Joe and covered the bullet's entry wound. She needed to stop air from getting in. She didn't know how she knew that. She just did. She then concentrated on the punctured lung. She instructed Joe's body to push the bullet fragments out of the lung. She heard a voice that seemed distant to her. "An ambulance is on the way."

Katie ignored the voice and continued working. She worked on repairing the lung. She just needed to get the lung functioning again. Once Joe could breathe properly, he could finish the repair himself. She heard the voice again, "Are you okay?"

Katie held up a finger, and the woman stopped talking. She didn't want to be rude, but what she was doing was far more important than being friendly to a stranger, even if that stranger was there to help. She continued with repairs and soon heard sirens. The ambulance stopped just as Joe's breathing started to return to normal. Katie looked up and saw paramedics hurrying towards them. She stood up and let them do their jobs.

Several police cars showed up. By then, about a dozen people had gathered around Katie and Joe. The officers pushed their way through and asked the people to step back. One officer, a young man, said to Katie, "I've seen you before. Weren't you in the station the other day talking to Captain Garcia?"

"Yes. I'm Katie Novak, and that's my husband, Joe. We are friends with Gabe, I mean Captain Garcia."

"So what happened here?"

"I don't know. Someone drove by and shot at us."

"Did you see who it was?"

"I'm afraid not. I wasn't paying attention. My husband saw it, and he saved my life."

"Thank you," he said. "I'll let Captain Garcia know what happened."

"Thank you," Katie said.

Nearby, the woman who had called 911 was speaking with another officer. She told them she saw a blue sedan but could give no other information.

The paramedics put an oxygen mask on Joe and loaded him into the ambulance. Katie got in the back with Joe and asked, "Where are you taking him?"

"Jackson McCormick Hospital," he said.

"No. Absolutely not. Take him somewhere else."

"Jackson McCormick is the closest hospital. We can't risk delaying treatment."

"Listen. The person who shot my husband may very well work at Jackson McCormick Hospital. I do not want to give him a chance to finish the job."

The driver, who had been listening, looked back and said, "We can go to Saint Genevieve. It's just a little farther."

"Yes. Go there. Thank you," Katie said.

Joe reached up and pulled the oxygen mask off. The paramedic grabbed it and tried to put it back on, saying, "You need this."

Joe pushed his hand away and said, "I don't need it. I'm fine."

The paramedic listened to Joe's chest with his stethoscope. After several seconds, he said, "That's strange. Your breathing sounds much better."

Joe held Katie's hand and said, "You did good back there."

Katie smiled and leaned over to hug him. "That's the third time this year I thought you were going to die, and April's not even over yet. You have to stop scaring me like that."

"I'm sorry, Katie. I'll try very hard never again to get shot, blown up, or run over by a car."

Katie noticed the paramedic's confused look and said, "It's an inside joke."

When they arrived at the hospital, the paramedics took Joe to the emergency room, where a doctor looked him over. She was relatively young, perhaps thirty-five, with long, dark hair tied in the back. She turned Joe on his side so she could examine his back. She was surprised that the entry wound had stopped bleeding and showed signs of healing. "When did this happen?" she asked.

"About thirty minutes ago," Katie said. "Maybe less."

The doctor looked at the wound again and said, "Weird."

She continued to examine Joe and the mark on his arm left by another of the shooter's bullets. It was mostly healed. "What happened here?" she asked.

Joe looked at the mark and said, "Oh, that? I'm embarrassed to say that I wasn't paying attention when my wife was curling her hair last week."

The doctor wrote something on her chart, saying, "Someone will be here shortly to take you to imaging. We need to get X-rays to see what we're dealing with."

She looked at Katie, who had blood on her clothes and hands, and called for a nurse. When the nurse arrived, she said, "Please show this young lady where she can wash up."

Katie returned five minutes later with clean hands. She and Joe were in a large room with other patients separated only by curtains, so Joe whispered to Katie. "I don't need to be here. I can take care of myself."

"I know you can, Joe, but we're stuck here now. If we leave, people will get suspicious."

"They are going to want to do surgery to remove the bullet fragments. I could do that myself now if I wanted to, but how could I explain that?"

"You can't. I'm afraid you are going to have to let them do the surgery and play patient for a couple of days. You'll be fine. You survived your hospital stay last time. You'll do it again."

There's something I need to tell you," Joe said. "The shooter wore a ski mask and a black leather jacket."

"What? Are you sure?"

"Yes. I'm sure."

"That means we might have been wrong about Holly being Virginia's killer."

"Maybe, but if she didn't kill Virginia, she was involved somehow. She might have been communicating with the killer. I don't know."

"Either that or there are two killers. Maybe they chose to dress alike to confuse potential witnesses."

"Whatever the reason, that person, or persons, are scared of us. They obviously want us to stop our investigation, either by killing us or intimidating us. They might try again. I don't want to put you in that kind of danger. Especially now that I have both you and our baby to worry about. Maybe we should go home and let Gabe figure this out."

"I share your concern, Joe, but I couldn't live with myself if someone else is murdered because we gave up."

The curtain opened, and an orderly stepped inside. "Okay, Mr. Novak, I'm going to take you to x-ray now." As he wheeled Joe out, he told Katie, "This shouldn't take long. You can wait in the waiting room. Someone will let you know what's going on."

Katie walked to the waiting room and found Gabe and Carmen there. They both stood up and hugged Katie. "How is he?" Gabe asked.

"He'll be fine. You know Joe. He's tough as nails."

"Yes, he is, but being shot in the back is serious."

"I guess he's just lucky," Katie said.

"He's more than lucky," Gabe said. That man is either superhuman or a guardian angel is watching over him."

"It seems you figured it out," Katie said. "We've tried very hard to keep it a secret, but I might as well tell you. Joe is one of the X-Men. He goes by the name 'SuperJoe.' I'm sure you heard of him."

Carmen laughed. "SuperJoe. That's funny."

"So, did you see who did it?" Gabe asked.

"I didn't, but Joe did. He said the shooter was wearing a ski mask and a black leather jacket."

"What? You're kidding."

"Nope. That's what he said."

Gabe thought momentarily and said, "If that's true, Holly might have been innocent."

"She may not have been the shooter, but she was not innocent."

"The shooter drove a blue sedan, just like Holly did. It's probably a different make, but he may also have been responsible for that hit-and-run. When you get back to work, find out what type of car Dr. Mechs drives. Oh, and his wife, too."

"I'll look into it, but I doubt the wife will be the culprit two cases in a row."

"Maybe not, but not discounting the wife is a lesson I only need to learn once."

They sat and talked for about ten minutes until the doctor finally entered the waiting room. Everyone stood up, and the doctor said, "Mrs. Novak. Your husband is being prepped for surgery now. He was fortunate. The bullet missed all his vital organs. It is fragmented, but all the pieces are close together and near the surface. They should be easy to remove. Honestly, I've never seen anything like it."

When the doctor left, Gabe said, "I'm gonna go with a guardian angel."

***

An hour and a half later, the doctor returned and said, "Mrs. Novak. The surgery went very well. Your husband will be fine. It will take about half an hour for the anesthesia to wear off, and then you can see him."

"Thank you so much," Katie said before the doctor left.

Gabe said, "We are glad Joe will be okay. Now that we know that, Carmen and I need to head home and cook dinner."

Katie hugged them both. "Thank you both for coming. I really appreciate your concern."

She waited another half hour until a nurse told her Joe was awake. She led her to Joe's room and left them alone. Katie hugged Joe and said, "That went smoothly. You see. Doctors aren't so bad."

"It went smoothly because I made it easy for them, with your help, of course. You did a good job back there. Maybe you should be the healer."

"I learned from the best," Katie said.

"More like the only."

"The only one now. I like to think that you won't always be the last Healer. Who knows how many people out there have Healer DNA? If two of them were to get together and have children, we might see another Healer in this world."

"You may be right, but considering those people left their village and scattered around the world, it could take hundreds, maybe thousands of years for that to happen. It would be like rolling a double six ten times in a row."

"You may be right, but there are billions of people rolling the dice."

"I guess if you look at it that way, it seems much more likely."

There was a knock at the door. Katie and Joe turned and saw Ashley come inside. She hugged Katie and then hugged Joe. "How are you feeling?" she asked.

"I'm fine," Joe said.

"Of course you are. So now you have to play patient like I did."

"That's pretty much the truth," Joe said.

"Okay, I have to tell you. This is not entirely a personal visit." She walked to the door, opened it, and motioned for someone to enter.

Bob Martin came in holding a news camera.

"Oh, no," Katie said.

"Oh, yes," Ashley said. You did it to me. It's my turn."

"I didn't know you were ready to return to work."

"Are you kidding? I'm not going to sit around the house when I'm perfectly capable of doing something productive."

"Ashley talked me into what she calls 'payback,'" Bob said. "She also talked me into running the camera. Hopefully I won't screw it up."

"You'll be fine," Ashley said.

"If it's that easy, why do I pay you so much?"

"It's not that easy. I just have confidence in your intelligence, Mr. Martin."

"Good comeback," Katie said.

"If it's okay with you, can we get started?" Ashley asked.

Katie looked at Joe and then back at Ashley. "I suppose it's only fair, but what about my clothes? I have blood on them."

"Don't worry about that," Bob said. "That will make it more real for the viewers."

Katie sat on the bed next to Joe. Ashley stood next to Katie. She picked up a microphone as Bob put the camera on his shoulder and started recording. "Hello, Milwaukee. This is Ashley Taylor. I have temporarily changed roles and stepped out from behind the camera to talk to my very dear friends, Katie and Joe Novak. Earlier today, Katie and Joe were shot at by a drive-by shooter not far from the Art Museum. Joe was shot in the back and is lucky to be alive today. Can you tell us what happened, Katie?"

"Sure. Joe and I were walking together. I wasn't paying much attention. Suddenly, Joe grabbed me, picked me up, and carried me away from the street. I had no idea what was going on until I heard the shots. That was when we both fell. I got up and saw Joe lying there. I knew he had been hit. I was afraid he was going to die. Fortunately, there was a jogger nearby who called 911."

"That must have been very traumatic for both of you. Do you know who shot at you?"

"I didn't see him, but Joe did."

Ashley held the microphone in front of Joe and said, "Joe, can you describe the shooter?"

"Well, I don't think I should tell you on camera. This kind of concerns you."

"It does? How does it concern me?"

Joe looked at Katie, who shrugged. "Okay. The shooter was wearing a ski mask and a black leather jacket."

Ashley let the hand that was holding the microphone fall to her side. She turned to Bob Martin and ran her other hand across her neck to indicate she wanted him to stop filming.

Bob made circles with his right index finger, indicating he wanted her to keep going.

She picked up the microphone again and said, "So does this mean the woman you caught didn't kill my mother?"

"We believe she was an accomplice in your mother's death," Katie said. "We now have our doubts she was the actual shooter."

"So, what will you do now?" Ashley asked.

"Our main concern is Joe getting better. After that, we'll see."

"Okay. Thank you, Katie and Joe, for speaking with us today. We wish you the very best. This is Ashley Taylor for Channel 23 News."

When they finished, Katie said, "Make sure no one mentions which hospital we are at."

"Why? Do you think this person might try again?" Bob asked.

"It's possible," Katie said. "I'm not too worried, but why make it easy for him?"

"Do you think it's a him?" Ashley asked.

"I'm not sure. It could be."

"I think it's a man," Joe said.

"Why is that?" asked Bob.

"Someone suffocated Holly Johnson with a pillow. It wouldn't be enough for that person to be stronger than Holly. That person would have to be much stronger. Anyone in that situation would summon every ounce of strength to stay alive. It would take a lot to overcome that."

"You have a good point," Bob said.

"If my mother's murderer is still out there, we need to find the son of a bitch," Ashley said.

"Gabe is still on the case," Katie said. "He's checking on something for us. We might know more when he gets back to us."

"I'm sorry, Katie," Ashley said. "I didn't mean to put pressure on you. I know you have your own problems. I just feel frustrated right now."

Katie put her hand on Ashley's arm and said, "I understand. I promise we will do our best to ensure this person pays for what he did."

"I know you will, Katie, but despite what I said, losing you would be much worse than not catching the killer. If you feel your life is in danger, then I would much rather you give up and go home."

"We'll be careful," Katie said.

"I think Ashley has a point," Bob said. "The killer obviously has your number. He wants you off this case. Maybe you should go home after Joe recovers. I mean, I would love to be able to show the city that one of our own caught another killer, but I would never want you to risk your life for a story."

"I appreciate that, Bob. We'll consider it."

"Okay," Bob said. "We need to get back to the station so we can get this on the tube at six."

When Ashley and Bob left, Katie said, "I'm starving. We never ate lunch today."

"I'm hungry too. Maybe you can ask someone to bring us some food."

"This isn't exactly a hotel with room service, but I will try."

Katie left the room and found a nurse. She told the nurse her husband hadn't eaten since breakfast, and the nurse said she would have something sent to him. Katie returned to Joe's room and waited. Twenty minutes later, a woman came up with a cup of clear broth.

"Can't you bring him some real food?" Katie asked.

"I'm sorry," she said. "He is on a clear liquid diet. Doctor's orders."

As the woman left, the doctor entered the room. "Hello, Mr. Novak. How are you feeling?"

"I'm fine. I'm definitely well enough to eat real food."

The doctor looked at his broth and said, "I'm sorry. It is a precaution after surgery. Sometimes, anesthesia can make people sick. She did a quick examination of Joe, checking his eyes, his temperature, and his blood pressure. She then listened to his lungs. "You are probably the healthiest gunshot victim I have ever seen. I'm going to cancel the clear liquids order. I can have some real food sent up, but to be honest, none of it is very good." She looked at Katie and said, "The cafeteria is still open. You might be better off picking up something from there and bringing it up here. It will be quicker that way, too. They make a good roast beef sandwich."

"Will somebody give me a hard time if I bring food up here?"

"I'll make sure they don't."

"Okay, doctor," Katie said. "Thank you."

The doctor looked at Joe and said, "I'll check on you later. If nothing changes, I think you will be ready to go home tomorrow."

When the doctor left, Katie went to the cafeteria and brought back two roast beef sandwiches. As they ate, her phone rang. She saw it was Gabe, answered it, and put it on speaker. "Hi, Gabe."

"Hi, Katie. How's Joe?"

"I'm fine," Joe said.

"Of course you are. Maybe someday you'll tell me how to get my own guardian angel."

"If I have a guardian angel, he or she is doing a terrible job of keeping me out of trouble."

"I can't argue with that," Gabe said. "I'm calling because I learned what Dr. Mechs and his wife have for cars. The Doctor has a white BMW 430i, and his wife has a red Ford Mustang convertible."

"Damn," Katie said. "I thought we were getting close. Is anyone else on the selection committee from that hospital?"

"No. Just Dr. Mechs. We need to look closer at our other suspects. I have someone doing a DMV check on all of them. I should know something soon."

"Okay, Gabe. Thanks for letting us know."

"Before we hang up, Gabe, I'd like to ask a favor," Joe said.

"Anything. What is it?"

"Katie's clothes are back at the hotel, but I don't want her to return there alone. I don't know if the killer knows where we are staying, but it's not worth the risk. Is there any way you can have an officer escort her?"

"Of course. I'll do it myself."

"No," Katie said. "I don't want to be there alone. I'd rather stay here."

"Maybe you can pick up clothes for both of us and bring them back here," Joe said.

Katie nodded and said, "Okay. That will work."

"I'll pick you up in about half an hour," Gabe said.

"Thank you so much, Gabe," Joe said.

***

Katie waited twenty minutes and then went downstairs to meet Gabe in the parking lot. She didn't want to keep him away from his wife too long, so she thought meeting him outside would speed things up. When Gabe arrived, Katie noticed his wife, Carmen, was in the passenger seat. She got in the back and said, "Hello, Carmen. I wasn't expecting you. I wanted to meet Gabe down here so he could hurry up and get home to you."

"We just finished dinner at home, and I thought it would be nice to take a ride with my man." She looked at Gabe and smiled.

"I appreciate both of you for doing this. I didn't want to tell Joe this, but the thought of returning to the hotel alone scared me a bit."

"That's understandable," Gabe said as he drove out of the parking lot. "Someone just tried to kill you, and they're still out there. That would make me nervous, too."

"I wouldn't be nervous," Carmen said. "I would be terrified. I worry about Gabe every time he goes to work, but thankfully, no one has tried to kill him yet. If that ever happened, I would want to leave town and move to Montana or something."

"I think you should reconsider leaving town," Gabe said. "Let the police handle this case. We are trained to protect ourselves. Do you even know how to use a gun?"

"No, but Joe does. He was in the Army."

"That's interesting. I didn't realize that. Where did he serve?"

"In Africa," Katie said before realizing her mistake. She couldn't exactly tell them he was fighting the Germans in World War II. She also had no idea if the U.S. Army had bases in Africa.

"Where in Africa?" Gabe asked.

"I don't know. He just said he was in Africa."

"Really? He didn't tell you all about his Army days?"

"He rarely talks about it."

"Didn't that concern you?" Gabe asked. "I mean, if he never talks about it, maybe something terrible happened over there. He might need psychiatric help."

"You know Joe, Gabe. He's not crazy."

"I don't think he's crazy, but he may have mental issues that need to be addressed."

"He has no mental issues. Trust me on that," Katie said.

Carmen put her hand on Gabe's knee. When he looked at her, she shook her head ever so slightly.

"Okay, but I still think you should go home until we catch this guy. I would hate to see anything happen to you."

"I appreciate your concern, Gabe."

When they arrived at the hotel, they all walked up to the room together. Katie gathered some clothes for herself and Joe and put them in a small bag. She added some toiletries and said, "Okay, I got what we need."

They returned to the hospital, and Gabe dropped Katie off near the front entrance. "Don't hesitate to call if you need anything else," he said.

"Thank you both so much," Katie said as she got out of the car.

Katie returned to Joe's room and found him watching television. "You're watching TV? That's a first."

"I was bored. I have nothing to read here. Do you know they have a station that shows nothing but the weather?"

"Really? That's interesting, Mr. Van Winkle."

"Very funny," Joe said as he turned off the television. "Did you get what you needed?"

Katie held up the bag. "I did. I also might have said something stupid."

"Really? What did you say?"

"The conversation with Gabe led to guns. I told him you knew how to use one because you were in the Army. He asked where, and without thinking, I said Africa, but I couldn't tell him where in Africa. To make a long story short, he now thinks you might have some unresolved mental issues."

"I think you made that long story too short. I can't imagine how it went from not knowing where in Africa to me having a mental illness."

"I don't know. It just did. The how is not important. I just don't want Gabe to think that you're crazy."

"Don't worry about it. Gabe's a smart man. He's had his doubts about me for a while, and my getting shot only made him more suspicious. Whatever you said is minor in comparison."

There was a reclining chair next to Joe's bed. Katie sat on it and reclined all the way back to test it out. It didn't lie flat like a bed, but it was close. "I hate that you have to stay here tonight," Katie said. "This will be the first night we haven't slept in the same bed since you got out of the hospital the first time."

"You can lie up here with me," Joe said. "There might be room."

Katie got off the recliner and lay next to Joe on the bed. The bed was small, and it was a tight squeeze, but there was enough room. Katie lay on her side above the covers with all her clothes on. She didn't want it to be awkward if a nurse came in. She put her arm around Joe and said, "I hope we never sleep apart."

Chapter 14

The doctor returned the following morning to examine Joe. "I wish all my patients recovered as quickly as you. I'm going to release you. Finishing your paperwork should take about an hour, and then you can go home."

When the doctor left, Joe and Katie took turns putting on clean clothes in the bathroom. A few minutes after they dressed, there was a knock on the door, and Gabe stepped inside. "How are you feeling, Joe?" he asked.

"I'm fine. They are releasing me shortly."

"I can't say I'm surprised," Gabe said. "I checked the cars owned by all of our potential suspects, and nobody owns a blue sedan. I then learned that a car matching your description was found abandoned three blocks from where you were shot."

"Did you find out who owns the car?" Katie asked.

"We did, and here is where it gets interesting. The car was owned by Richard Weiss. He apparently committed suicide by jumping off a four-story apartment building. I don't know how it got past the officers investigating the case, but he didn't live in that apartment building. In fact, he didn't live anywhere. He was homeless."

"Homeless?" Katie said, surprised.

"Yes. He lived in his car. He was also the first homeless person that we know of to donate an organ since Holly Johnson switched jobs."

"So what happened to his car after he died?" Joe asked.

"No one knows," Gabe said. "The fact that he owned a car must have slipped under the radar."

"So whoever pushed him off that roof must have taken the car and used it as a way to prevent being identified," Katie said.

"That's what we think. Holly Johnson probably never killed anyone, although we believe she was still part of it."

"We think so, too," Katie said.

"I did learn one other thing that is kind of disturbing," Gabe said.

"What's that?" Katie asked.

"I learned that Joe was never in the Army, like you said. Why would you lie about that, Katie?"

Katie looked at Joe and back at Gabe. "I didn't lie to you, Gabe. I promise you that. It's just difficult to explain."

"Joe's records are spotty at best. He has no credit cards, no vehicles, and no bills of any kind in his name. Everything seems to be paid through a trust set up by his grandmother. Even the house you two bought was paid for with money from the trust. Why would she do that for Joe and not her other grandkids? In addition, I called his high school, and they have no record of Joe Novak attending school there."

"I changed my name," Joe said. "I was in the Army under the name 'Joe Young.'"

"You did more than change your name, Joe. You erased your former existence. Why? Are you running from the law?"

"Please, Gabe," Katie said. "Joe is a good man. Let it go."

"I can't let it go, Katie. You should know that. I took an oath to uphold the law."

"I think we need to tell him," Joe said.

"Are you sure?"

"Yes. You tell him. You are better at explaining than I am."

Katie looked at Gabe, but nothing came out.

"What do you want to tell me?" Gabe asked.

"This is going to sound very far-fetched at first, but hear me out. Many years ago, in a small village in Northwestern Croatia, there lived a line of people known as Healers. Once or twice a century, a healer was born. The healer was blessed with a special and unusual gift. He had the ability to heal himself and others."

"You mean like a medicine man?"

"No. These Healers were nothing like medicine men. They could feel what was going on inside their bodies at all times. If they had an infection, a tumor, or some other illness, they knew about it and could consciously instruct their bodies to combat whatever was ailing them. They could also use this gift to heal quickly from any non-fatal injury. In addition, through a simple touch, they could feel inside other people and heal them as well."

"You're right. That does sound far-fetched. What does this have to do with Joe?"

"I'm getting to that. During the First World War, the village where the Healers came from was destroyed, and the last Healer was killed. The survivors scattered. One survivor, a pregnant woman, made it all the way to The United States. She died while giving birth the day the ship docked in New York. They found a letter on her."

Katie scrolled through the photos on her phone and found the English translation of the letter. She gave her phone to Gabe and said, "This is the English translation of the letter."

Gabe read the letter. When he got to the part about the name the mother wanted for her baby, he said, "Josip Novak? Is this a relative? Like a great-grandfather?"

"No. Joe said. That letter is about me. I was born in the hospital on Ellis Island on the third day of October 1916. I was in the Army and fought the Germans in Africa during World War II. The grandmother that you refer to is actually my daughter. When I changed my identity, I put all my investments in her name."

Gabe was silent for a few seconds and then let out a big laugh. "You had me going there for a minute."

"If I can prove it to you, will you promise never to tell anyone? If word got out, my life, our lives, would become extremely difficult. They might even lock me up to do experiments on me."

Gabe's face turned serious. "You really believe this. Don't you?"

"I do, and you will too, once you give me your word."

"Okay. If you can prove it, I won't tell anyone."

Joe stood up, held out his hand, and said, "Give me your hand."

Gabe hesitated momentarily and then held out his hand. Joe held it and said, "This will probably be the weirdest thing you've ever felt. It's okay. Try not to freak out."

Joe concentrated, and soon, they were connected. "Holy shit!" Gabe said before letting go of Joe's hand. "What the hell just happened?"

"We were connected," Joe said. You should have been able to feel what was going on inside your body as well as what was going on inside me. It is nothing to fear. Let's try again. This time, concentrate on what you are feeling."

Gabe put his hand out, and they were soon connected again. Gabe could feel his internal organs. He could feel his heart, his lungs, and his kidneys. He could feel Joe's internal organs as well. It was as if they were one person. "This is incredible," Gabe said. "I don't know how, but I can feel everything."

Joe was silent for about 30 seconds and then said, "You are pretty healthy, Gabe, but I did find one thing that could be a problem in the future. Do you feel it?"

"I do feel something that's off, but I'm not sure how to describe it."

"I have been feeling this my entire life, so it's natural for me, but I can see how difficult it would be for you to understand. After a while, you will get used to it. Just ask Katie."

"So, what's wrong? What is it that I feel?"

"You have a kidney stone. It's not bad now, but it will worsen if we do nothing."

"What can you do?" Gabe asked.

"I can tell your body to break it up, which I am doing right now. Do you feel it?"

"I do. I feel it. This is amazing."

Joe let go of Gabe's hand and said, "You might feel a little pain the next time you pee, but that will be the end of it."

"That was truly something else. I believe you now, but I don't understand how it is possible."

"I honestly don't know, either, Gabe. I just know what I can do."

"So, how have you stayed young after all these years?"

"Aging is like a disease. I simply treat it like any other disease. I stop it before it starts."

"That is quite a gift you have there, Joe. I see now why you can recover so quickly. I just don't understand. If you can heal yourself, why are you in the hospital?"

"It would be difficult to explain refusing treatment after I got shot."

"I see your point. Is that what happened the last time you were in the hospital?"

"No," Katie said. "That time, Joe used all his energy to save me. He might have died if the paramedics hadn't shown up when they did."

"When this is all over, I would like to learn more about this thing that you can do, but right now, we have a killer to catch. I will see if I can learn more about where that blue sedan has been. When you leave here, maybe you can think of another angle to investigate. Perhaps you can look deeper into our possible suspects and see if you can find a connection that we've missed so far."

"We will certainly try," Katie said.

"Just be careful," Gabe said. "Don't do anything stupid like walking into a building rigged to explode."

***

When Gabe left, Katie e-mailed Billy and asked him to look at the social media accounts of their suspects. She asked him to check for photos of a person wearing a black leather jacket.

Soon, someone came to their room with several forms for Joe to sign. Joe didn't have health insurance for obvious reasons, but now he was presented with a large hospital bill. He had the money to pay for it, but now thought he should have refused the ambulance ride to the hospital. What's the worst that would have happened? A few people would have thought him crazy, but he would have been forgotten after a few days.

On the other hand, some eager young reporter, like Katie used to be, might have picked up on the story and looked into it further. Ultimately, he figured it was worth the money if he could stay in the shadows. Unfortunately, he couldn't keep his secret from Gabe, but avoiding the hospital would not have prevented it.

When the hospital finally released Joe, they took a cab back to their hotel. It was a little late for breakfast and a little early for lunch, but they hadn't eaten all day and were hungry. They decided to go to the hotel restaurant before returning to their room. They ordered breakfast, and as they were waiting for their food, Joe asked, "What do you want to do? Should we stick it out or cut our losses and go home?"

"Are you worried?"

"Of course I'm worried. Someone tried to kill us, and that person is still out there. I can live with not finding a killer. What I can't live with is losing you."

Katie put her hand on Joe's. "That is very sweet, but if we give up now, I will live the rest of my life with regret. I'm sure you don't want that either."

"No, I don't. If we are going to stay, we must be vigilant."

"The best defense is a good offense," Katie said. "The sooner we find this killer, the sooner the danger will pass."

After breakfast, they returned to their room. As soon as Joe closed the door, Katie hugged him tight. "I don't know if I told you, but I am so happy you're okay."

"Thanks to you."

She let go and said, "Let me see your wound."

Joe turned around and lifted his shirt. Katie removed the bandage and ran her finger over a small scar that had almost disappeared. "A scar is like a memory, but this one will soon fade away."

"Maybe the scar will fade, but not the memory." He turned and put his hands on Katie's face. "I will never forget that I am still here because of you."

They kissed, and soon the passion flared again. Joe picked up Katie and put her on the bed. Katie laughed and said, "Should you be exerting yourself? You just got out of the hospital."

Joe got on top of Katie, kissed her, and said, "This is exactly what I should be doing. Doctor's order. She said I should get plenty of sex."

"Rest. She said you should get plenty of rest."

"That's not what I heard."

"Of course it isn't, you dirty old man."

An hour later, a notification sound came from Katie's phone. She got up, found her phone, and checked the message. It was an email from Billy with a photo attached. It was a screenshot of a social media post. The profile name was Brennan Robertson. It was a photo of him and Holly Johnson standing beside each other. Both were smiling and wearing identical black leather jackets. The caption read, "My bestie and I bought new jackets today." The post was from three years ago.

"It looks like we found our killer," Katie said.

Joe got out of bed and walked over to where Katie was standing. She held out her phone, and Joe looked at the photo. "Well, what do you know? The question now is, how do we prove it? I mean, owning a leather jacket is not a crime."

"I don't know. Hopefully, we'll think of something." Katie said. She then replied to Billy. She thanked him and asked if he could dig deeper into Brennan

Robertson. "Look for anything related to homeless people or organ transplants." After that, she forwarded the email to Gabe.

They showered together and then got ready to go out. What do you want to do now?" Joe asked.

"I'd like to talk to Robertson, but that will lead nowhere. I asked Billy to dig up information on him. Let's learn more before we do anything."

"That's reasonable," Joe said. "So, do you want just to hang out here?"

"No. Let's go to the news station. I want to check in and see how Ashley's doing."

"Okay. It will be good to get out for a while."

***

When they arrived at the television station, they entered the newsroom and walked past Debbie's desk. She grabbed Joe's arm to get his attention and said, "Hi, Joe. I heard what happened to you, and I'm glad it wasn't serious. I also wanted to thank you for what you did for me the other day, but the pain is starting to come back. Do you think you can do that pressure point thing again?"

Joe looked at Katie, who nodded. "Sure. I'm happy to help."

Joe held Debbie's forearm with both hands and randomly pressed it while working to fix the cause of the pain. After several minutes, he let go and asked, "How does it feel now?"

Debbie rotated her wrist several times and said, "It's much better. Where did you learn that technique? I Googled it but couldn't find anything about it."

"Google doesn't know everything," Katie said.

"You should look up how to prevent it from returning," Joe said. "I'm no expert on ergonomics. Maybe the company can get you a different desk or something."

"I'll look into it. Thanks so much."

They walked to Ashley's desk but found it empty, so they went to see Bob Martin. "I'm glad to see you out and about so quickly," he said to Joe as they entered his office. "I can't say I'm surprised, though."

"I told you he was tough," Katie said. "We thought we would see how Ashley was doing back at work, but I guess we missed her."

"She's on assignment. She took Andy with her. They should be back soon if you want to wait."

"How does she feel about Andy?" Katie asked. "He was about to take her job."

"No. I hired Andy before Ashley was shot. I wanted him to be a backup photographer. His main job will be in editing, but I want him to have some real-world experience in the field, too."

"I bet she's happy about that."

"Ashley does a good job. She knows I wouldn't replace her. What about you? Have you learned anything new?"

"Well, we know Holly Johnson was probably involved in Virginia Hall's death and the death of several homeless people, but she probably was not the killer," Katie said. "We think the killer was a nurse at the hospital named Brennan Robertson."

"Why do you think that?"

"Because Ashley and Joe were both shot by someone wearing a ski mask and ablack leather jacket." She held out her phone and said, "Billy sent this screenshot to me. Robertson posted this photo three years ago. He and Holly are wearing the same leather jacket. Since Holly is dead, the killer must be him."

"That's good work, but it's not proof."

"I know. We're working on it."

"Okay. Let me know when you learn something new."

When they left Bob's office, they went to Katie's desk. She was checking her emails when she heard Ashley's voice. She stood up, saw Ashley, and waved her over. Ashley hugged Katie and then Joe. "This is great," she said. "It feels like old times."

"I see you have an apprentice," Joe said.

"Oh, yes. Andy's doing a good job. So what brings you two here today?"

"We mostly came here to see how you were doing," Katie said.

"I'm fine. I needed to get back to work. So, have you learned anything new in your investigation?"

"We learned who might have killed your mom," Katie said.

"You did? Who is it?"

Katie took out her phone and showed Ashley the photo. "We're not certain, but we think it was this man. His name is Brennan Robertson. He is a nurse at the hospital you were in."

Ashley looked closely at the photo and said, "I remember him. That son of a bitch was in my room acting all friendly and shit as if he cared about me."

"You're lucky you were surrounded by people when you were at the hospital," Joe said.

"Oh, my God. You're right. Do you think he might still be after me?"

"I doubt it," Joe said. "You told us what you know. He's too late. The only thing he can do now is stop the people currently investigating him, which is us. Now that we know who he is, killing us won't help him."

"No, it won't, but he probably doesn't know what you know. You need to be careful. I still think you should go home," Ashley said. "The police can handle it from here. Even if they can't, I'd rather see that scumbag go free than to lose either one of you."

"We'll be careful," Katie said. "You don't have to worry about us."

When they finished talking, Katie and Joe walked to Billy's desk. "Hi, Billy," Katie said.

"Oh, hi, Miss, I mean, Hi, Katie. Hi Joe. I'm still working on your request, but I found something that might interest you."

"Oh, yeah? What did you find?"

"Robertson's parents divorced when he was ten. According to court documents, his father had a drinking problem and would become abusive when drunk. The mother got custody of Brennan, and she got the house during the divorce. Two years later, the father was homeless. He confronted Brennan's mother at their home and, after a lengthy argument, shot and killed her in front of the boy. He then shot himself."

"Oh, wow!" Katie said. "That would explain his hatred for homeless people. He probably assumes they are all like his father."

"He might also think he's doing society a favor by trading their lives for people he deems acceptable," Joe said.

"We can't let him continue to play God with people's lives," Katie said.

"I agree. Do you think we should go to his work and confront him? We can secretly record him. If we push his buttons, we might get him to confess."

"Don't you think that might be dangerous?"

"He already wants to kill us, and there wouldn't be anything he could do to us at the hospital in front of a bunch of witnesses."

"Okay. Let's go talk to a killer."

Chapter 15

As Katie and Joe were walking out of the news station, Katie's phone rang. She looked at the phone and saw it was Gabe. She hit the answer button, put the phone to her ear, and said, "Hi, Gabe."

"Hi, Katie. I was busy and just saw your email. I hope you guys are not planning on talking to Robertson."

"We're just leaving the station and about to head to the hospital right now."

"Don't do that. He's dangerous. We're going to pick him up for questioning."

"Okay, fine. We'll head back to the hotel."

They had reached Katie's car. She clicked the button to unlock it when an arm grabbed Katie around the neck. She screamed. She felt cold, hard steel pressed against her head. Joe was on the other side of the car and started to move when Brennan Robertson pressed the gun harder into Katie's head and said, "Don't move, or I'll shoot her."

Joe stopped, and Robertson said to Katie, "Hang up the phone and give it to me."

Katie hung up the phone and handed it to Robertson. He put it in his pocket and looked at Joe. "Get in the car."

Joe hesitated but got in the car.

Robertson opened the door and pointed the gun at Joe's head. He looked at Katie and said, "Don't try anything, or he gets it first." He then got in the back seat. "Your turn, Honey. Get in."

Katie got in the car and closed the door. "Give me your driver's license," Robertson said.

"My driver's license? What do you need that for?" Katie asked.

"You're not exactly in a position to ask questions. Just give it to me."

Katie handed him her driver's license. "Now yours," he said to Joe.

Joe pulled out his license and handed it to the man. He looked at both licenses and, surprisingly, handed them back. "I want you to leave the parking lot and turn right," he said.

Katie did as he told her and followed Robertson's directions across town. They ended up at a self-storage place. He instructed Katie to pull up next to a terminal and told her the code to open the gate. He then instructed her to drive straight ahead.

She drove almost to the back of the facility when Robertson told her to stop in front of a large storage unit. She put the car in park, and he told her to get out while he kept the gun pointed at Joe's head. He then got out, followed by Joe. He pressed the gun against Katie's back while he opened the lock and slid the door up.

"Get in," he said, following Katie and Joe inside. He turned on the light and closed the door.

The unit was half-filled with furniture. A musty, stale odor filled the room. "You won't get away with this," Joe said.

"We had a good thing going until you two got involved, but you will soon no longer be a problem."

"You and Holly were friends. Why would you kill her?" Katie asked.

"Holly was weak. She would have told the cops everything. I saved her from a horrible life in prison."

"I bet it was your own ass that you were more concerned with," Joe said.

"You can think what you want. I don't care."

"So, who else is involved?" Katie asked. "Is it Dr. Mechs?"

"Are you kidding? He's straight as an arrow."

"Really? Didn't you need his vote on the selection committee?"

"I might as well tell you since you won't be repeating it. Mechs could always be counted on to vote in the hospital's best interest, and saving the lives of people in the hospital was definitely in the hospital's best interest."

"So this was all just you and Holly?"

"Enough talking," he said. He pointed to Joe. "You. Turn around."

"You're going to shoot me in the back?" Joe asked.

"Just turn around. I'm not going to shoot you in the back. I have plans for you later."

Joe reluctantly turned around, and Robertson struck him hard on the head with the butt of his gun. Joe dropped to the ground, unconscious.

Katie screamed, but Robertson ignored her. He opened a dresser drawer and removed a bottle and a syringe. He filled the syringe with the liquid from the bottle. He set the bottle down, removed the air from the syringe, and said, "There is a young woman at the hospital named Bridget O'Malley who has a defective heart. I think you would like her. She is a lot like you. You are about the same size as her and have the same blood type. Your license also says you are an organ donor. What a happy coincidence. She is quite a special lady, and you will be happy to know you are helping her have a normal life."

"You are not injecting me with that," Katie said. "I will fight you."

"You can try, but you will fail and cause more pain for yourself."

"You're sick. I know about your father. He was sick, too. I guess the apple doesn't fall far from the tree."

"I'm sick? I'm the one helping humanity by saving people who deserve to have a chance at life."

"You're not God. You can't decide who deserves to live and who deserves to die."

"That's where you're wrong. That is exactly what I can do." He moved in close, grabbing Katie's left wrist with his left hand. He then turned and used his back to push her against the wall and hold her there. Katie tried hard to pull her hand away, but she wasn't strong enough. She tried beating on him with her right hand to no avail.

"Just then, Joe, who was still on the ground, grabbed Robertson's leg. He connected to him and quickly found his heart. He instructed the muscle to relax, which it did. It relaxed so much that the heart stopped beating. There was no pain. Robertson simply passed out after a few seconds with no oxygen going to the brain.

The door opened, and Gabe stepped inside, his gun drawn. Joe stood up and saw Katie with a terrified look on her face. He looked down and saw a needle sticking out of her arm. It was empty.

Joe had intended to revive Robertson, but now it was he who had to choose who lived and who died. For him, there was only one choice. He pulled the needle out of Katie's arm and held her with both hands. He needed to stop the drug before it reached her brain or the baby.

He first told her heart muscle to relax. It was a similar instruction to what he gave Robertson's heart, but Katie's heart only slowed. It didn't stop. Joe needed time to isolate the bad blood. When he found it, he diverted it past all her major organs and into the liver for detoxification. He then instructed her heart to beat at a normal pace again.

When he finished, he disconnected from Katie but still held her arms. "Are you okay?"

Katie hugged Joe tight and cried. "I thought we were both going to die."

Joe hugged her back and said, "I know. It's over now."

"I thought he knocked you out," Katie said.

"I told you I can heal myself even while I'm sleeping. I learned today that works when I'm unconscious, too."

Gabe bent down and felt Robertson's wrist for a pulse. Feeling none, he asked, "What happened here?"

"He wanted me to be his next organ donor," Katie said.

"I guess his heart couldn't handle the excitement," Joe said.

"I don't know what you did, but I'm certain he got what he deserved," Gabe said.

"How did you find us?" Katie asked.

"I was able to get a trace on your phone. Fortunately, he didn't make you throw it on the ground."

"I've lived a long time, and two things still amaze me: the height of human intelligence and the depth of human stupidity," Joe said.

"I don't think keeping the phone was stupid," Katie said. "I think throwing it out would have been suspicious. What was stupid was not turning it off."

"What was stupid was us not going home yesterday. Can we go home now?" Joe asked.

"Tomorrow," Katie said. "There are a couple more things we need to do."

Chapter 16

The next morning, Katie and Joe ate breakfast at the hotel for the last time. Before they checked out, they went back to the room so Katie could change her clothes. She put on a tight-fitting skirt and a low-cut blouse. They then drove to the news station.

Once inside, they took the elevator to the second floor, where the studio was located. Joe waited patiently while a makeup artist worked on Katie's face. He couldn't understand why that was necessary since Katie had already put on makeup that morning, but he knew the realities of the business.

When the news program started, Katie joined the morning news team to discuss the events of the last week. He was very proud of how calm and articulate she was. She did not utter one "um" during the entire conversation. When it was over, Joe hugged her and said, "You were great."

After leaving the news station, they drove to Jackson McCormick Hospital. Once inside, they asked for Bridget O'Malley's room and were directed to room 312. They took the elevator to the third floor and found her room. Before going inside, Katie asked, "Same as before?"

"Sounds good to me."

Katie knocked on the door and opened it. A young woman lay on the bed. Several wires ran from her chest to a machine monitoring her heart. She looked very similar to Katie. She was about twenty-five years old, with long dark hair. Unlike Katie, she had blue eyes, but Joe could see why her heart would have been a good match. "May we come in?" Katie asked.

"Sure. Come in. Do I know you?"

"No," Katie said. "My name is Katie, and this is Joe. What's your name?"

"I'm Bridget. Bridget O'Malley."

"It's nice to meet you, Bridget. We are from the Three Eagles Church of the Healer. We would like to pray for you."

Bridget shook her head and said, "No. Everyone I know has prayed for me. Look where that got me. Nowhere."

"What's wrong with you?" Katie asked.

"I had an accident on my motorcycle. A dog ran out in front of me. I swerved to avoid it, but ran into a picket fence. A piece of wood punctured my heart and damaged the muscle."

"So you are waiting for a new heart?" Joe asked.

"That's right, but I don't think it will ever happen."

"Sometimes God works in mysterious ways," Katie said. "I think you should give him one more chance and let us pray for you."

Bridget thought for a moment and said, "Fine. What do I have to lose?"

"That's the spirit," Joe said. "We are going to hold your hands and pray silently. Is that okay?"

"Sure. Go ahead."

Katie and Joe stood on opposite sides of her and held her hands. Joe connected with her and could feel the damage to her heart. He immediately got to work healing the muscle. After ten minutes, the woman said, "I think that's enough praying."

Joe let go and looked at the monitor. "Look," he said. "Your heart is beating stronger. I think it's working."

Bridget looked at the monitor and was shocked at what she saw. "Oh, my God."

"Give us five more minutes," Joe said. "We are almost there."

Bridget held out her hand, and Joe connected with her again. After five minutes, he let go and looked at the monitor again. "I think you're going to be okay."

"She looked at the monitor again and asked, "Who are you?"

"We are just two people who want to make a difference," Joe said.

"Did God send you?"

Katie and Joe looked at each other, and Katie said, "We have to go. It was very nice meeting you."

When they left her room, Katie said, "I'm surprised you were able to fix her heart so quickly."

"It's not completely better. I fixed the major issue, but it would take much more time to get her to a hundred percent. She will never be able to participate in strenuous activity, but it's good enough for a normal life. As a very wise young woman once told me, I can only do what I can do."

"Even so, that felt good. We should focus on helping people like Bridget. I don't want to investigate murders anymore."

"I totally agree."

Just then, Katie's phone rang. She saw it was Michael and answered it. "Hi, Michael."

"Hi, Katie. Is Pops with you?"

"He's right here. Just a minute." She hit the speaker button and said. "You're on speaker."

"Hi, Pops. I'm sorry to interrupt what you are doing there, but we have a problem at the resort."

"What kind of problem? What happened?" Joe asked.

"Someone was murdered."

I truly appreciate you taking the time to read Last Rites. I hope you enjoyed following Katie and Joe on their latest adventure.

I would be incredibly grateful if you left a review on Amazon, Goodreads, or wherever you purchased this book. Your thoughts help other readers discover the series and mean a lot to me as an author. Whether it's a few words or a detailed review, your feedback makes a difference.

Thank you again for your support. I couldn't do this without readers like you.

Charles Huss

Books In This Series

Last Healer Mysteries

Joe, a reclusive, ageless centenarian, meets Katie, an ambitious news personality with dreams of being an investigative reporter. Together, they solve crimes and explore the full potential of Joe's healing abilities while navigating the complexities of their intimate relationship.

Book One - The Last Healer

On the eve of her thirtieth birthday, Katie, a television news reporter, unhappy with her career and her love life, decides to spend the weekend alone at a Wisconsin ski resort.

Joe is a man content to live a private life in his cabin in the woods. Since the death of his wife, he has avoided intimate relationships and prefers to keep a low profile to prevent people from learning of his unusual abilities.

On the way to the ski resort, Katie makes a wrong turn during a snowstorm and hits Joe with her car. Lost and with no cell signal, Katie tries to keep Joe alive until she can get help. During Joe's recovery, Katie learns his secret and soon helps to investigate his family's mysterious past while Joe helps Katie investigate a double murder. Love blossoms while they slowly unravel both mysteries, but danger lies ahead. Can Joe discover the full extent of his abilities before it is too late?

Book 2 - Last Rites

In this gripping sequel to "The Last Healer," Katie and Joe, fresh from their honeymoon, must race to Milwaukee to save the life of Katie's dear friend Ashley after she and her mother fall victim to a ruthless attack. With Ashley on the brink of death while a priest delivers Last Rites, her only chance for survival is Joe's remarkable healing powers.

What starts as a rescue mission turns into a murder investigation as they investigate the killing of Ashley's mother. While searching for the shooter, their investigation leads them to a chilling conspiracy centered on the city's homeless population. As they uncover more of the truth, they become targets as someone is determined to silence them. Will Katie and Joe find who is behind a series of murders, or will they become the next victims?

Book 3 – Last Chance

In Book Three of the Last Healer Mysteries, Katie and Joe, after deciding to quit investigating murders, are thrust back into it when a man is murdered at Joe's resort.

The victim is no ordinary man. He is a suspected jewel thief, believed to have hidden stolen jewels at the resort. While they struggle to handle all the treasure seekers, Katie and Joe debate how involved they should be in the murder investigation. They don't know the killer lurks in the background, taking orders from some of the most powerful people in Wisconsin while he waits for Katie and Joe to find what he is looking for.

Book 4 – Last Flight

In Book Four of the Last Healer Mysteries series, Katie and Joe witness the deadly crash of a prototype aircraft and save the life of one of its occupants. After Joe discovers evidence of sabotage, Katie insists she can investigate the crime despite being almost nine months pregnant.

Someone planted an explosive device in the aircraft, killing the company's founder and jeopardizing the struggling startup's future. Was the attack meant to destroy the company, or was it something more personal? As Katie and Joe hit one dead end after another, they discover the killer isn't finished. With time running out, they race to save the next victim, but with people dying, a murderer on the loose, and Katie in labor, what's a Healer to do?

Other Books By Charles Huss

Truth Be Told

Peter Beckett awoke 25 years ago with no memory of his past. Since then, he's been haunted by a gift he never asked for and doesn't want. People can't lie to him. To Peter, it feels like a curse that has left him isolated and feared by all who get to know him. Only his priest accepts him for who he is.

The FBI has been watching him, and they need his unique talent to track a deadly drug cartel that has infiltrated Milwaukee, fueling a dangerous spike of fentanyl overdoses. Rookie agent Hannah Meyers is assigned to recruit Peter, who is reluctant to help, but is intrigued by Hannah after she lies to him.

As the investigation deepens, details of Peter's former life emerge. With secrets unraveling and lives on the line, Peter must decide whether to return to the glorious life he once knew or give it all up for love.

Saving Apollo

Apollo is no ordinary dog. Along with his sister, Athena, he was genetically modified to be smarter than a chimpanzee. When the lead geneticist quits over a dispute about the fate of the dogs, chaos erupts, and Apollo escapes, ending up on a small island off the Florida coast. There, he befriends twelve-year-old Ethan, who has just moved to the island with his dad, Ryan.

As they uncover Apollo's extraordinary ability to understand them, they also learn about the perilous fate that awaits him if he returns. With the help of their neighbor, Brooke, a local veterinarian, they devise a plan to save Apollo and Athena. Standing in their way is Jack Strauss, a former Marine and head of security at the lab that created Apollo and Athena.

"Saving Apollo" is a heartwarming, family-friendly story of friendship, love, and compassion.

Falling Star

A meteorite crashes into the serene wilderness of a national park. In its aftermath, both people and animals succumb to aggressive behavior followed by death. Two rookies, FBI agent Beth Hartley and Park Ranger Mike Bauer, are put together to investigate the strange events.

Beth is tough as they come on the outside but vulnerable on the inside. After her last breakup, she has given up on men to focus on her career. Mike, a former military police officer, has developed trust issues and prefers his new career where he has no partner that he needs to rely on.

As their investigation brings them closer to the truth, they find themselves getting closer to each other. In a dangerous forest where every animal is a potential threat, and even the air could be toxic, their best chance for survival is a partner they can trust.

Identity Crisis

After Alex Neumann agrees to participate in his father's groundbreaking memory recording experiment, he awakens years later to find he is not the man he used to be. He soon becomes a pawn in a deadly scheme involving a ruthless businessman, an Army general, and the President of The United States.

As Alex peels away layers of deception, his true identity slowly emerges, along with skills foreign to his old self. He will need all those skills and the help of friends he meets along the way to survive and turn the tables on his adversaries.

Bad Cat Chris: The Baddest Cat You'll Ever Love

When Chuck volunteered to help a local cat shelter clean cages one morning, the last thing he expected was a kitten climbing up his back to perch on his shoulders, but that was the beginning of a relationship that would test the limits of human endurance and compassion.

This is the story of Chris, a cat like no other who would turn the lives of Chuck and Rose upside-down while eventually showing them that bad can be good and love can come from the most unlikely places.

This book is based on Chris's blog at BadCatChris.com and is a collection of sometimes serious but mostly humorous stories about the ups and downs of living with a bad cat.

About The Author

Charles Huss was born and raised in the suburbs of Chicago but has lived most of his adult life in the Tampa Bay, Florida, area. He is a graduate of St. Petersburg College and is the writer of several books. He currently lives with his wife, Rose, and their three cats.

Don't miss out!

Visit the website below and you can sign up to receive emails whenever Charles Huss publishes a new book. There's no charge and no obligation.

https://books2read.com/r/B-A-LHRY-VYEBD

BOOKS 2 READ

Connecting independent readers to independent writers.

Did you love *Last Rites*? Then you should read *Last Chance*[1] by Charles Huss!

In Book Three of the Last Healer Mysteries, Katie, and Joe, after deciding to quit investigating murders, are thrust back into it when a man is murdered at Joe's resort. The victim is no ordinary man. He is a suspected jewel thief, believed to have hidden stolen jewels at the resort. While they struggle to handle all the treasure seekers, Katie and Joe debate how involved they should be in the murder investigation. They don't know the killer lurks in the background, taking orders from some of the most powerful people in Wisconsin while he waits for Katie and Joe to find what he is looking for.

Read more at charleshuss.com.

1. https://books2read.com/u/bQlaZE

2. https://books2read.com/u/bQlaZE

About the Author

Charles Huss was born and raised in the suburbs of Chicago but has lived most of his adult life in the Tampa Bay, Florida area. He is a graduate of St. Petersburg College and is the author of several books. He currently lives with his wife, Rose, and their two cats.

Read more at charleshuss.com.

www.ingramcontent.com/pod-product-compliance
Lightning Source LLC
Chambersburg PA
CBHW021919170626
46807CB00007B/2897